Happy Birthday, Mr Darcy

Victoria Connelly

Cuthland Press

Copyright © 2013 Victoria Connelly

www.victoriaconnelly.com

Victoria Connelly asserts the moral right to be identified as the author of this work.

Cover image by Roy Connelly

Published by Cuthland Press

This paperback edition first published 2013

Ebook edition first published 2013

ISBN-13: 978-0-9569866-7-2

To my lovely friend and fellow writer, Jane Odiwe,
with love.

.

ACKNOWLEDGMENTS

Once again, I'd like to thank all my dear readers who have stayed with the adventures of the Austen Addicts. I love hearing from you all and I really hope you enjoyed this latest story. And thank you to my dear husband, Roy, for putting up with yet more Jane Austen research!

* * *

'Anything is to be preferred or endured rather than marrying without affection.'

Jane Austen in a letter to Fanny Knight, 1814

* * *

CHAPTER 1

Katherine Roberts was quite determined to keep calm. It was just a wedding. There was nothing to worry about. The fact that it was her own wedding and that it had never been in her grand plan to get married was quite beside the point. She would remain calm and gracious at all times like Anne Elliot or Elinor Dashwood – two of the most controlled of Jane Austen's heroines.

Still, as she sat in her tiny book-lined office at St Bridget's College in the heart of Oxford, the early evening light gilding her long dark hair and turning the papers on her desk golden, she found it hard to believe that, in a week's time, she would be married.

Katherine smiled to herself as she twisted the engagement ring on her finger. Warwick had chosen a stunning Georgian ring from the late eighteenth-century set with a single rose-cut diamond. The stone was oval in shape and how it sparkled! Katherine held it up to the light now to admire its beauty. It wasn't garish like some modern diamond but rather infused with the magic that age brings and seemed almost silvery in complexion which Katherine knew was due to the foil backing of the stones which was typical of jewellery of the time.

It thrilled her to know that her ring had been around in Jane Austen's time. Indeed, it was possible that her idol had seen it. Perhaps she'd been walking by a jeweller's with her sister, Cassandra, when she'd spied the ring and stopped to admire it. Katherine liked to imagine that – a direct, physical link with her favourite author.

Still, she couldn't help thinking that it was much too good a ring for her to wear every day. She'd never worn anything more ornate than a Russian wedding ring before Warwick had proposed to her and, for the first few weeks, she'd been very self-conscious about wearing it to her lectures and tutorials but had been secretly delighted with the attention it had got from her female students who had fawned over it with gasps of wonder and romantic sighs.

For a moment, she thought back to Christmas at Purley Hall and the last Jane Austen conference she'd attended with Warwick. It had snowed and snowed until there'd been no hope of any of the guests leaving until well after the festivities were over unless it was by police escort like the dastardly Jackson Moore or by helicopter like dear Doris Norris. Katherine had spoken to her friend just the week before and was glad to hear that she was fit and well and learning to take things easier.

'I've had to spend a lot of time on my sofa,' Doris had told Katherine, 'and what else is there to do but reread my favourite books and watch all my favourite adaptations again? I fear the BBC video of *Pride and Prejudice* is on its last legs! The lake scene is looking very wobbly these days.'

'You'll have to buy it on DVD,' Katherine told her. 'It will last longer.'

'On PVC?'

'No, DVD.'

'But I've only just got the hang of video. Oh, dear. I guess I'll never be able to keep up with things. I wonder what Jane Austen would have made of it all. I mean, fancy being able to watch Mr Darcy on TV and make him fast forward and rewind at the touch of a button. It's quite extraordinary, isn't it?'

Katherine laughed. 'When it comes to Mr Darcy, I rather prefer the pause button myself!' They giggled like a couple of school girls.

Ah, yes, that was something which had been worrying Katherine. Would she be able to fully indulge in her evenings sitting on the sofa, wearing her baggy Fairisle cardigan and eating peppermint creams whilst watching Jane Austen adaptations? As long as she could remember, this had been a very private and uninterrupted pleasure of hers but what would happen when she was sharing a home with Warwick? How would he feel if she needed to escape into the early nineteenth-century for a couple of hours? They'd watched a few films together of course but it was different when you were dating because you were always impeccably behaved, weren't you? But what would happen after you'd been living together as husband and wife for a few weeks, a few months. A few *years*?

'You're not watching that film *again*, are you, Katherine? Honestly, I know you lecture in Austen but do you really need to keep watching the same Colin Firth and Alan Rickman scenes over and over again?'

Katherine tried to blink the scene away. They wouldn't be like that, would they? They were both Janeites; they had an understanding about such things and Warwick was partial to the young Kate Winslet in *Sense and Sensibility* and he'd also expressed a naughty fondness for Hayley Atwell's Mary Crawford in *Mansfield Park* so they were bound to tolerate each other's little obsession, weren't they?

Sometimes, Katherine had to pinch herself at the speed at which things were happening. It didn't seem that long ago since she had been writing letters to her favourite author - Lorna Warwick. She remembered with great fondness sitting at the little table by the window in her cottage. It was a table not dissimilar to the one at the Jane Austen House Museum where the author used to write her novels. Katherine would make a cup of Earl Grey tea in a blue and white china mug, take her favourite fountain pen from her study desk and give herself the luxury of time to handwrite her letters to the historical novelist. Only the historical novelist had turned out to be a man - a man with whom she had fallen deeply in love.

Who would have thought it? The academic and the romantic novelist? Her work colleagues at St Bridget's College had split into two camps: those who thought that the match was absolutely delicious and those who were simply appalled and showed their disdain by keeping their distance which suited Katherine fine because, like Elizabeth Bennet, she could not abide a snob.

Besides, Jane Austen's novels were full of odd couples. Who would have paired the outspoken Elizabeth with the dour Mr Darcy? Well, readers would have, obviously, for opposites always attract in fiction but imagine their modern counterparts in real life. And think of the young, Emma and her Mr Knightley, and wilful Marianne and steadfast Colonel Brandon. The novels were littered with couples one would never have thought to pair. So why not Katherine and Warwick? If there was one thing that the novels of Jane Austen taught us it was that love was idiosyncratic, unpredictable as well as rather wonderful.

To be absolutely fair, Katherine really didn't care what people thought about her and Warwick even though there'd been a bit of press about their engagement.

'*Lorna and Katherine – Happy Ever After?*' Ran the saucy headline in the tabloid *Vive!*. They'd somehow managed to find out that she and Warwick had been pen pals before they'd met and accused Warwick of 'cruel duplicity' but other publications were kinder with headlines such as '*Romantic Novelist Writes His Own Happy Ending*' and '*Jane Austen Love Match*' which was Katherine's personal favourite.

Warwick had told her that she would have to get used to a bit of press intrusion.

'I'm not J K Rowling,' he told her, 'but they do occasionally poke their noses into things and want an interview.'

That didn't worry Katherine but there were other things worrying her about their marriage. Up until now, her books and her teaching had been everything to her but marrying Warwick was bound to change that. The day to day business of living with somebody was going to shift her focus away from herself and her work and she wasn't sure how that was going to affect her. And Warwick too. She'd never been around him when he was fully immersed in his writing. What if he turned into some kind of beast – slamming his study door shut and locking her out of his life? Would she be able to cope with the working Warwick?

So far, they had only grabbed weekends and brief holidays together and they'd both been on their best behaviour around each other – putting their work on the backburner and giving each other their undivided attention. Well, except when inspiration struck and Warwick had to scribble some note down about his latest hero or heroine. But that couldn't last, could it? You couldn't carry that momentum forward into everyday married life and that thought terrified Katherine for she'd never lived with a man before. Her time had always been her own.

Then there was the practical side of things like where would all their books go? Would they have separate bookcases for their individual collections or were married couples expected to join their libraries together? What if it all became one big literary jumble and she could never find her beloved volumes again? It was very important to Katherine that she could put her hand on a particular volume at any time especially when she was writing her own books and needed to reference a specific title. Would that sense of order be lost once she was married?

They'd once had a conversation about their vast book collections.

'How many do you think you have?' Warwick had asked her.

Katherine had pursed her lips together and her head did a succession of little nods as if she was counting them in her mind's eye.

'About four thousand, I think.'

'Right,' Warwick said, completely unfazed.

'And you?'

Warwick's dark eyes had widened. 'Well, I've never actually counted them but if you've got four thousand-'

'Approximately.'

'Approximately,' he said, 'I must have at least *ten* thousand. If not more.'

Katherine gasped.

'An editor friend of mine recently moved house and he had to use the same firm of removal men who did the British Library,' Warwick said.

Thinking about all those books made Katherine's head spin. It would be wonderful to be surrounded by fabulous volumes, of course, and to share Warwick's library but she feared the sheer number of books at the same time. There was only one solution. They would have to find the right house that was big enough to house their mammoth library without making it feel as if the book-lined walls were closing in on them.

She bit her lip nervously at the thought of a new home and then thought of her much-loved little Oxfordshire cottage and of the comfortably snug rooms, the woodburning stove and the modest pieces of antique furniture she'd collected over the years. It was a home she'd been so happy in but it was time to say goodbye to it now and move forward to a new home with Warwick.

Warwick was going to sell his beloved house. When he'd first suggested it, Katherine had been heartbroken and had tried to persuade him to change his mind. She couldn't bear the thought of never seeing The Old Vicarage again with its beautiful sash windows and lofty ceilings but Warwick seemed adamant.

'I love The Old Vicarage, of course I do,' he'd told her, 'and I'll miss it like crazy but it's part of my past and it's time now to move forward and find a home together. Who knows – there might well be its double in some corner of Oxfordshire.'

Katherine felt lucky that Warwick was willing to make the move to her part of England because she couldn't imagine a life away from Oxford.

'I can write anywhere,' he told her and so they'd registered with several Oxfordshire estate agents and had viewed two properties together already.

It was fun to imagine the kind of property they'd end up with. They'd decided that it had to be bigger than Katherine's but smaller than Warwick's. Georgian or Regency would be perfect with the generously proportioned rooms of the period and the large sash windows that they both adored but Katherine also leaned to earlier properties with their cosy little rooms and beams.

'Too dark,' Warwick had said when she'd told him. 'And don't say I can write by candlelight. I want nice big windows in my study.'

Katherine took a deep breath. She was going to live with Warwick Lawton – *really* live with him - not just for the space of a weekend or a holiday but forever.

Gazing down at the silvery brightness of her engagement ring, she realised that her life was about to change out of all recognition and that thought terrified her. What if she was making a huge mistake?

CHAPTER 2

'What a pity Cassandra isn't old enough to be a bridesmaid,' Robyn Love Harcourt said wistfully as she tidied away the bridal magazines which her boss, Dame Pamela Harcourt had ordered. There were quite a few of them and each one had been plundered for ideas in preparation for the upcoming wedding. Robyn, who was a true romantic, had spent hours flipping through the pages and she couldn't stop imagining her daughter in a fondant-pink dress, throwing rose petals down the aisle.

'She'll be old enough one day,' Dame Pamela said. 'Maybe I'll get married again and she can be *my* bridesmaid.'

Robyn blinked in surprise, unsure if Dame Pamela was joking or not. She looked at her boss for a moment as she pulled out a ten by eight glossy black and white photograph of herself in the role of Ophelia in *Hamlet* before signing it with a flourish.

'There, send that out to Mr Piper,' she said.

Mr Piper was one of Dame Pamela's biggest fans and regularly wrote her passionate letters that ran to ten or more pages. He sent her flowers on her birthday, chocolates for Valentine's Day and outrageously lavish gifts from his home furnishings company for Christmas. He was, Robyn thought, Dame Pamela's number one fan but she did often wonder what he did with all the photographs she kept posting to him. He could probably paper his whole house with them by now.

'Would you really consider getting married again?' Robyn asked.

Dame Pamela looked up from her desk. She was wearing a powder blue dress with a silk scarf tied around her neck and an enormous pair of aquamarine earrings. Her silver-white hair was swept up in its famous chignon and a large diamond clip sparkled in its depths.

'My dear Robyn, I have had more husbands than I care to count and, although I adore men, I'd prefer not to live with one again. Apart from Higgins, of course.'

'Of course,' Robyn said with a smile, thinking of the faithful butler who had been a part of Dame Pamela's life for at least twenty years.

'Anyway, *you* are going to look absolutely resplendent in your outfit,' Dame Pamela told her.

Robyn smiled, thinking of the Regency dress which had been specially made for her in her role as maid of honour. It was an Empire-line dress in sky-blue – one of Katherine's favourite colours – and was hand-embroidered with white roses which both Robyn and Katherine were going to carry in their bouquets. Finished with a simple white ribbon around the waist, the dress really was the last word in sophistication and Dame Pamela had also insisted on a matching Spencer jacket being made in case the English summer proved inclement. Robyn adored her outfit and couldn't wait to wear it. She knew it would be treasured for years to come and worn again and again at Purley Hall's Jane Austen conferences when the time came to dress up.

Robyn stared out of the window of Dame Pamela's office, her gaze going far beyond the cedar tree towards the fields. Dan was out riding that way on Perseus. He'd taken Biscuit the Jack Russell with him but dear old Moby the Golden Labrador was sitting at home in his wicker basket after a more sedate walk in the grounds earlier that morning. He was slowing down and knew his limitations but he still enjoyed a poke around in the hedgerows and Robyn's pace with the baby stroller suited him just fine.

For a moment, Robyn thought of her tall, handsome husband. He was Warwick's best man and was going to wear the most perfect Regency gentleman's outfit with a sky-blue cravat to match her gown. She had only seen him in it once at the last fitting and had almost had to ask for some smelling salts for fear of swooning completely. He looked like he'd just stepped out of the pages of a nineteenth-century novel.

'Robyn?'

Robyn blinked and looked at Dame Pamela. Had she said something?

'You were miles away,' Dame Pamela said.

'Just thinking about the wedding,' Robyn said, feeling herself blush.

'Thinking of our Danny in his Regency finery, were you?'

Robyn couldn't hide her smile. 'It's very hard not to,' she said.

Dame Pamela nodded. 'Why don't men dress like that anymore?' she said, her heavily-powdered forehead wrinkling in consternation. 'I mean, you can't beat a nice cravat, can you?'

'Or a waistcoat,' Robyn added.

'But men insist on wearing those awful sweatshirt things with the hoods or a baggy T-shirt that does nothing for the male form.'

'Higgins does his best,' Robyn said.

Dame Pamela nodded. 'Higgins has done his utmost to resurrect the waistcoat but he's no Colin Firth, alas.'

Robyn giggled.

'Let's just hope we can persuade a few of the male guests to don a costume.'

Robyn nodded. Dame Pamela was going to wheel her great wardrobe of Regency costumes out for guests to rummage through and she'd had at least two dozen new ones made especially for the occasion in the hope that everybody would join in. Yes, Dame Pamela was quite determined that Purley Hall was going to be awash with muslin, bonnets and cravats come the day of the wedding.

CHAPTER 3

Warwick Lawton had lost his pen and was bent double with his head upside down when the telephone rang. He ignored it for a moment because the pen was his favourite and he simply had to find it. It was a fountain pen which Katherine had bought him and he used it for signing contracts and letters to his readers and for writing the very first outline of a new novel which he'd been in the middle of doing when the pen had gone missing. He couldn't bear the thought of losing it.

Fountain pens were a bit of a private joke between the two of them because he had bought her one for her birthday engraved with the words 'So much in love' from *Pride and Prejudice* and she had had his fountain pen engraved with the words 'A great proficient' also from *Pride and Prejudice*. Warwick had erupted with laughter when he'd read it.

'You didn't go for *"so much in love"*, then?' he'd asked with a naughty grin.

'No,' Katherine had said. 'I like to be original.'

The phone stopped ringing and blissful silence filled the study once more. Warwick picked up some loose pages of A4 paper on his desk but the pen wasn't there.

For a moment, he looked at the silver-framed photograph of him and Katherine which he kept on his desk. It had been taken by a passing rambler up in the Peak District when Warwick had taken Katherine rock climbing. They had their arms wrapped around each other and their smiles couldn't have been bigger if they'd fallen into the plot of their favourite novel like in the TV drama *Lost in Austen*.

He smiled as he remembered the day. They'd driven up to Derbyshire from Katherine's cottage in Oxfordshire. Warwick had bought an enormous hamper filled with gourmet food and they'd spread a tartan rug out on the ground overlooking the glorious countryside of the White Peak. Then he had introduced her to his world of ropes, harnesses and carabiners. Katherine had been uncharacteristically quiet.

'Nervous?' he'd asked her.

'Of course not,' she'd said. 'I'm just concentrating.'

He smiled at her sun-filled face in the photograph now. The soon-to-be Mrs Lawton.

'Mrs Katherine Lawton,' he said, the name sounding luxurious on his tongue. Although she was still to be Dr Katherine Roberts at St Bridget's and would publish her books and papers under her old name too. But this beautiful, intelligent, funny woman was going to become his wife and he couldn't quite believe his luck.

The phone started ringing again and he picked it up. 'Yes?' he said abruptly.

'Darling! Whatever is the matter?'

'Nadia,' he said with a weary sigh. 'You've caught me at a bad time.'

'And when is a good time? You were meant to be calling me about this new idea of yours.'

'Yes, I know. I'm trying to get it down right now only I've lost my pen,' Warwick said, pulling extension lead of the phone as far as it would go so he could inspect the rest of the room. Honestly, his agent had the most uncanny knack of catching him at the worst possible moment as well as being able to stick her foot in it like nobody else he'd ever met.

Warwick had come pretty close to parting with Nadia Sparks after the stunt she'd pulled at Purley Hall during that first fateful Jane Austen conference he'd attended. His agent had had one too many drinks and had then gone and told Katherine about Warwick's secret identity before he'd got a chance to tell her himself.

'You'd still be waiting to tell her if it hadn't been for me!' she'd said in defence of herself.

Anyway, that was all ancient history and Katherine had forgiven him. Eventually.

'I can't tell you how much I'm looking forward to this weekend,' Nadia went on. 'How's the groom holding up?'

'The groom is holding up fine,' Warwick said, raking a hand through his dark hair. Why did everybody keep asking him that? Were they expecting him to do a runner or something?

'No cold feet?' Nadia pressed.

'No,' Warwick said.

'No last-minute regrets about losing your bachelor lifestyle?'

'Nadia – are you trying to put me off marriage?'

'Well, I *am* concerned that being an old married man might restrict your literary output,' she said.

'It's not going to affect my writing,' Warwick told her.

'Well, maybe not now but what will happen when little Warwick junior makes an appearance?'

'What?'

'Babies!'

'Oh, Nadia! We're only just about to become husband and wife. Give us a chance!'

'It's you who's always telling me that "a lady's imagination is very rapid" and mine is more rapid than most,' Nadia said.

'Indeed it is!' Warwick said. 'Look, you *will* be on your best behaviour at the wedding?'

'I'm *always* on my best behaviour,' Nadia said with a fruity chuckle.

'Just stay clear of the cocktails.'

'Warwick, darling. You know I never drink these days.'

Warwick rolled his eyes at the blatant lie.

'Anyway, enough about weddings,' Nadia said, getting down to business, 'I thought you were going to send me this synopsis you've been talking about before you swan off on your honeymoon.'

'I am. I will,' Warwick said, 'as soon as I can find my pen.'

'Pen?' Nadia said. 'You write it with a *pen*?'

'I always write the synopsis with a pen and then type it up later.'

'Good heavens! I didn't know my best client was living in the dark ages.'

'I like a nice pen,' Warwick said. 'It helps me think things through – the slow flow of ink onto the page-'

'Just get it to me before all this wedding business takes over, okay?'

'I'll get it to you,' Warwick said, hanging up. It was then that he spotted the pen. It had somehow rolled off his desk and onto the floor and had gone under a cabinet on the other side of the room. He bent down to retrieve it, his hair flopping over his eyes. He'd been going to get a nice short haircut but Katherine had asked him to keep it long for the wedding.

'It looks cute,' she'd said. 'Like 'Hugh Grant in *Sense and Sensibility*.'

Warwick flicked it out of his eyes now and looked at the engraving on the pen again.

'*A great proficient*,' he read with a little laugh. 'A great idiot more like. What on earth is someone like Katherine doing marrying a chump like me?'

CHAPTER 4

'2013 is a very special year. Can anybody tell me why?'

'It's the year you're getting married, Dr Roberts,' Bethany, a dark-haired student said, and everybody laughed.

Katherine was taking her last tutorial of the summer term with twelve students and all of them had clocked the diamond engagement ring as soon as she'd started wearing it and had beaten her down with questions.

'Well, yes,' Katherine said, 'I can't deny it's special because of that but why else? What are we celebrating?'

'The year after the Olympics?' another student offered.

Katherine was in too good a mood to throw one of her Lady Catherine de Bourgh glares at her student.

'Have a look at the frontispiece,' Katherine said.

A couple of her students looked blank.

'The front page,' Katherine elaborated. 'This edition has a facsimile of the original frontispiece. What do you notice about it?'

'It doesn't have her name on it,' a student called Laurie volunteered.

'That's true,' Katherine said, thankful that somebody had made a half-decent observation, 'but look at the date.'

'1813,' Bethany said. 'It's two hundred years old.'

'Exactly,' Katherine said. '2013 marks the two hundredth anniversary of *Pride and Prejudice* and what I thought we could discuss today is what makes a story live on centuries after it was written. Why are we still reading and studying Austen, the Brontës, Dickens and Hardy?'

'Because they wrote good stories,' Bethany said.

'But what makes them good?' Katherine asked.

'The characters,' Laurie said. 'They feel - like - modern.'

Katherine grimaced at Laurie's use of the word 'like' but she, at least, was engaged in the discussion, unlike some of her students.

'Rupert,' she said, picking on a handsome boy who was staring out of the window watching as a pair of pretty girls waltzed by the grass in the quad.

'Yes?' he said, raising his sleepy eyes to her as if in surprise at seeing her there.

'Do you have any thoughts about it?'

He looked totally lost for a moment and Katherine kept him suspended in torment for a moment longer before releasing him.

'Stories survive not just because of empathetic characters that we can still identify with but because the author has something to say to us and they have the ability to communicate that to the reader in a clear and often amusing way. Jane Austen knows how to hook a reader with her endearing and often infuriating characters but she also keeps us hooked by her wit, her observations, and her unique use of language. Lots of other writers had books published at the same time as Jane Austen and yet they've been lost to us. Austen has survived because she has a unique voice. But the themes she explores are also important.'

Rupert was staring out of the window again.

'What themes does she explore, Rupert?'

His head snapped back to face Katherine, his skin a scary white. Katherine watched as the hopeless student flipped through the pages of *Pride and Prejudice* as if the answer to her question would leap out at him at any moment. If Rupert Browning-Danes read only the same number of chapters each day as the number of pints he drunk each night then he wouldn't be floundering half as much, Katherine thought. Honestly, didn't some of these students realise that she was feeding them the finest that English literature had to offer?

She thought of her dear friends at Purley Hall and how they would gasp in horror if they knew that these students hadn't even bothered to read half the books on their syllabus. She often wondered why students chose a subject like literature if they didn't really like reading. But perhaps Rupert was one of those students who would come back to Austen later in life and think, hey – I missed out on a treat here. She could only live in hope.

'Love,' Rupert suddenly blurted out, startling Katherine.

'Yes, love is a theme which Jane Austen explores in all her novels.'

'Marriage,' Rupert added, getting into his stride.

'Good,' she said. 'Love and marriage.'

'Dr Roberts?' a student called Clara said. 'Do you think humour works for readers in different times?'

'Why do you ask?'

'Well, we're reading *Love's Labours Lost* with Mr Bradley and he keeps telling us it's a comedy but I don't find it very funny at all,' Clara said. Clara was well-known for her straight face and Katherine doubted very much if anything would ever tickle her fancy.

'Well, what do you think? Take a character like Mr Collins,' she said. 'Can't any age find him amusing?'

'I just think he's rather annoying,' Clara said with a little sneer.

'Perhaps that's something we can explore later but, going back to the themes of love and marriage – are they always linked in *Pride and Prejudice*? Do they always go hand in hand?'

Bethany shook her head. 'I don't think Mr and Mrs Bennet are in love anymore and Charlotte Lucas doesn't marry for love, does she?'

Katherine shook her head. 'That's right. Marriage was often a matter of survival for women in Jane Austen's time and Charlotte Lucas knew that Mr Collins's proposal was probably the only one she'd get and that she'd have to take it. Love was a luxury.'

Laurie giggled. 'Thank God we don't have to marry in order to survive now. Marriage is a matter of personal choice. Like yours.' She said with a sweet smile. 'You're marrying for love, aren't you?'

Katherine smiled. 'Yes,' she said. 'I'm marrying for love.'

At the end of the day, Katherine tidied her desk, handed out all the marked essays and the reading list for the holidays and left St Bridget's College clutching a huge bouquet from the English department. She drove home, leaving Oxford behind her for the duration of the summer and, once she got home, she kicked off her shoes, poured herself a glass of white wine and sat in a pink and green striped deckchair in her garden with her two cats, Freddie and Fitz, for company. She then ran a hot bath, read three chapters of the latest Lorna Warwick novel which she'd been eking out so as not to finish it too quickly, and then she went to bed. Tomorrow was a very important day.

Katherine caught a taxi from the train station in Bath, smiling at the golden-hued buildings of the Georgian town and the streets which Jane Austen would have known so well. Her mind spiralled into her favourite literary worlds and she thought of Catherine Morland and Isabella Thorpe discussing hats and ribbons, and of Anne Elliot and Captain Wentworth falling in love all over again.

She wished with all her heart that her timetable allowed her more time for she longed to walk through the streets and squares, a copy of *Persuasion* in her handbag and copy of *Northanger Abbey* in her hands. But she promised herself enough time to pop into the Jane Austen Centre before she caught her train back to Oxford. But this wasn't just any trip to Bath and now wasn't the time to be a tourist.

The taxi left the bustle of the city centre behind and headed up into the hilly suburbs until it reached 6 Southville Terrace. It was a very pretty honey-coloured house with an enormous bay window overlooking a tiny garden. It was in a wonderful situation being within easy reach of the centre of Bath but also close to the countryside in a part of town which Jane and her sister Cassandra would have known well from their extensive walks. Katherine loved it.

She paid the driver and got out of the taxi, walking up the little pathway and ringing the bell of number 6. A moment later, a young woman in her mid-twenties opened the door. She had a shock of Marilyn Monroe-blonde hair and a huge lip glossed smile.

'Katherine! *Katherine!*' she cried, her arms wide and embracing.

'Shelley. How lovely to see you.'

'Come in! *Come in!*' Shelley said. She had a tendency to say everything twice when she was excited.

It had been Dame Pamela's idea to get in touch with Shelley Quantock. She was a friend of Mia Castle's and Mia had told Dame Pamela all about Shelley's wonderful costumes at the Christmas conference and Dame Pamela had commissioned some new ones for the wedding from the talented seamstress in Bath.

'How *are* you?' Shelley asked as they entered the hallway. 'Getting nervous?'

'No,' Katherine said. 'Everybody keeps asking me that but I'm not nervous at all about the wedding.'

'Just about marriage in general, eh?' Shelley said with a laugh.

Katherine swallowed hard, not daring to tell Shelley that she was rather close to the mark with her last statement.

'MIA!' Shelley suddenly shouted. 'Katherine's here!'

There was the thunderous sound of footsteps as Mia ran down the stairs, her dark hair flying out behind her and her eyes shining brightly. She was followed by a huge chestnut dog who hurtled into the hallway at top speed, skidding on the tiled floor and crashing into their visitor.

'Oh, *Bingley!* Sorry, Katherine,' Mia said as she pushed the bouncing dog out of the way and embraced Katherine.

It was then that Katherine became aware of a strange smell that seemed to be coming from no room in particular – a blend of ylang ylang oil and peppermint tea, Katherine thought, or maybe peppermint oil and ylang ylang tea – she couldn't quite be sure.

'Would you like a cup of tea?' Shelley asked.

'Say no!' Mia blurted. '*Never* drink a cup of tea in this house!'

'It's all right!' Shelley said. 'I wasn't going to offer her Daddy's latest. It's absolutely foul and stains your teeth green. I must tell him before he starts to market it.'

'Shelley's dad runs Quantock Teas,' Mia said, 'and he tries out his new blends on Shelley. They're usually lethal to the taste buds and deathly to the nose.'

Katherine smiled. 'Maybe I'll just have a glass of water.'

'Very wise,' Mia said.

Shelley opened a door from the hallway into the front room where a large man with long hair sat in a chair reading a book called *Oils for Love and Life*.

'Katherine's here for her final fitting, Pie,' Shelley said. 'We'll be upstairs, okay?'

Pie grunted something from out of the depths of the chair without looking up from his book and Shelley closed the door.

'He doesn't say very much, does he?' Katherine said, frowning.

'No,' Shelley said, 'but he has very talkative hands and your mind would boggle if you knew what he could do with a bottle of almond oil.'

Katherine caught Mia's eye and the two of them grinned.

'Come on,' Shelley said, 'I can't wait to see you in your dress.'

CHAPTER 5

The three of them went up the stairs followed by Bingley who was anxious not to miss out on anything.

'I'll shut him in your bedroom, Shelley,' Mia said, catching hold of Bingley's collar and marching him into one of the rooms off the landing before shutting the door firmly on him. 'You do not want paw prints on your wedding dress!'

They entered a tiny but perfect room that was full of fabric.

'This used to be Pie's room but – well – he's in mine now,' Shelley said with a naughty smile. 'Don't tell Daddy, though. I don't think he'd approve. For one thing, he'd expect me to squeeze another tenant in here and this room's too important for our business now, isn't it?'

Mia nodded. 'Since Dame Pamela ordered all those costumes, we've been non-stop. Word gets around so quickly in the Austen community and Shelley's probably one of the most sought-after costume designers in the country.'

'Well, I don't know about that but business is definitely booming,' Shelley said. 'We're practically full-time now although I still do three days a week at Tumble Tots and Mia's still auditioning, aren't you?'

'Still waiting for that lucky break!'

'Tell Katherine about the part you've got,' Shelley said, her face lighting up with a huge smile.

'What?' Katherine said.

'Well, I've got a small part in a BBC drama due out next year.'

'Really? That's marvellous!' Katherine said.

'And she has to sing too!' Shelley said like a proud

mother.

'Oh, congratulations,' Katherine said, giving Mia a hug.

'Well, it's just a small part.'

'Yes, like Marilyn Monroe's in *All About Eve*,' Shelley said with a wink. 'You'll *totally* steal the show!'

'I'm sure you will, Mia. It's great news. I'm so excited for you,' Katherine said.

Mia smiled. 'Gabe's really thrilled. He won't stop talking about it. Last week, we were doing our weekly shop and he went and told the cashier!'

Shelley and Katherine laughed.

'Oh, you must come and say hello to him,' Mia said. 'He wants you to sign your book for him.'

'I'd be happy to,' Katherine said, her hand reaching out to touch a beautiful satiny dress in a lovely apple-green. Her eye then caught a row of bright ribbons and she gasped. This whole room was a feast for the eyes, she thought.

'It's so cruel that a bride only gets to wear one dress when there are so many wonderful fabrics to choose from,' she said.

'Well, I'm not stopping you from buying more dresses,' Shelley said, 'but I would like to point out that I'll only have four days in which to make them.'

'Best that I just stick to the one, then,' Katherine said with a reluctant sigh.

'And here it is,' Shelley said.

Katherine turned to see the dress which had been hiding behind a beautiful old-fashioned dressing screen which Shelley had covered in scraps of vintage wallpaper.

Mia sighed in delight as Shelley brought it out for Katherine whilst the bride-to-be merely gazed in silent wonder.

The dress was a perfect column of white chiffon which gave it a wonderfully fluid quality and it was unimaginably soft to the touch. The wide square neckline was pretty but modest and the sleeves were long and trimmed with lace. Scalloped detailing at the bottom made the dress look as if it was dancing and it was finished with a pearl-white ribbon under the bust. It was simple and unostentatious – just as Katherine had asked. Not for her were the Marie Antoinette-style gowns with skirts wider than the average church aisle nor the cleavage-skimming, no-sleeve gowns that left so little to the imagination. She wanted elegant, beautiful and simple.

White wasn't the prevalent colour for wedding dresses during Jane Austen's time. Many chose darker colours which would make it much easier to use the dress again afterwards but Katherine liked the idea of white and Warwick thought that a white wedding was the most romantic thing he could think of.

Still unable to speak, Katherine was helped by Shelley and Mia as she tried the dress on and, a couple of minutes later, they gasped in amazement at the vision before them.

'Are you comfortable?' Shelley asked. 'Nothing too tight or too loose anywhere?'

Katherine shook her head.

'Oh, Katherine! You look amazing. Straight out of a novel,' Mia said.

Shelley smiled, her eyes wide and filled with wonder at her creation. 'You've brought the dress to life,' she said.

Katherine turned around and dared to look at her reflection in the full-length mirror on the wall opposite. Her long dark hair looked almost Pre-Raphaelite against the pure white of the dress. She was planning on wearing it threaded through with ribbons and white roses on the big day but, today, it was loose and unadorned – just as Warwick liked it.

It was then that something strange happened. Katherine's eyes filled with tears which overflowed and spilled down her pale cheeks.

'Katherine!' Mia cried, instantly by her side.

A great sob left Katherine.

'Oh, my goodness!' Shelley said, leading Katherine towards an old wooden chair, pushing off the scraps of material which were strewn across it.

Katherine sat down and the crying continued for a few moments with Shelley and Mia exchanging anxious looks.

'Is it the dress?' Shelley said. 'Is there something you don't like?'

Katherine shook her head. 'I love the dress,' she said.

'Are you not feeling well?' Mia said. 'Can I get you a cup of tea? From next door – not from here – that would only make you feel worse.'

Shelley nudged Mia in the ribs.

Katherine shook her head again. 'No thank you,' she said, giving a loud sniff. 'Oh, goodness! What is wrong with me? I *never* cry. Well, apart from when my cat Freddie cut his paw on a broken bottle, and that moment in the *Sense and Sensibility* adaptation when Marianne thanks Colonel Brandon when he's about to leave her room.'

'Oh, well,' Shelley said, 'we *all* cry at that!'

'I just feel so emotional,' she said. 'I don't know what's wrong with me.'

'Brides-to-be are *meant* to be emotional,' Mia said, kneeling down beside her. 'It would be odd if you weren't.'

'Really?' Katherine asked, mopping her eyes with a tissue which Shelley had handed to her and taking a deep breath.

'Truly,' Mia said.

'I feel so silly,' she said.

'You're not silly,' Shelley said. 'You probably just need a good night's sleep.'

They were quiet for a moment with just the occasional sniff from Katherine and the gentle thump of Bingley's nose against Shelley's bedroom door as he tried to get out.

'You're not having second thoughts, are you?' Mia asked gently, taking hold of Katherine's shaking hand.

Katherine shook her head and pushed a dark wave of hair out of her face.

'No, of course not.'

'Then it's probably just nerves,' Mia said. 'Like when I was about to have Will. I wanted him – of course I did – but it didn't stop the nerves about going into labour and-'

'*Please!* Shelley said. 'No Technicolor details – we get the idea!'

'Yes, nerves,' Katherine said, nodding as if in agreement.

'And nerves are good,' Mia said. 'For an actor, nerves mean a great performance because you care about the job you're doing. You want to do well. Maybe it's the same for you – you're nervous because you care – because the day is important to you.'

Katherine looked up and smiled at Mia. 'Maybe you're right.'

'Trust me – it's nothing more than that.'

'Here,' Shelley said, 'let's get you out of the dress.'

'Yes,' Katherine said. 'I wouldn't want to stain it with my tears.'

A few minutes later, Katherine was back in her navy and white polka dot dress and her tear-stained face had just about returned to normal.

'Okay now?' Mia asked and Katherine nodded. 'How's about coming next door for a real cup of tea?'

Gabe was sketching in a notebook when Katherine walked in but quickly put it down and stood up to greet her.

'Great to meet you at last,' he said, shaking her hand.

'And you too,' she said, instantly recognising what Mia had seen in him. He was tall with strawberry-blond hair and a kind, open face and Katherine liked him instantly.

'And congratulations on the upcoming wedding,' he said.

'Thank you.'

'I'll make the tea,' Mia said, disappearing into the kitchen.

'So,' Katherine said, 'you're really into Jane Austen?'

'I really am,' Gabe said. 'Mia made me read all the novels and I'm just working my way through the letters now. They're wonderful.'

Katherine's eyes sparkled with pleasure. A man who adored Jane Austen was a rare creature indeed.

'And, of course, I've read your book,' he said.

Katherine beamed with pleasure.

'Which I'm hoping you'll sign for me.'

'I'd be delighted.'

Gabe reached across to the coffee table on which sat a pristine copy of *The Art of Jane Austen* and Katherine took a pen from her handbag – the fountain pen on which was engraved *'So much in love'* – and signed Gabe's book.

'And this is Mia's son?' Katherine said, noticing a photo frame on one of the bookcases.

'That's our Will,' Gabe said, smiling proudly.

Katherine smiled too. 'He's adorable,' she said, taking in the rosy red cheeks and a head full of dark curls just like his mother.

Mia entered the room with the tea. 'So, you've spied our little angel, have you?'

'Mia, he's absolutely gorgeous!' Katherine said.

'And he'll have a little cousin before too long,' Mia said.

'Yes, how's Sarah?' Katherine asked, remembering Mia's older sister.

'Getting larger by the minute,' Mia said. 'Honestly, she looks as if she's about to explode.'

'Darling, it's not really surprising. She is due in a couple of weeks,' Gabe said.

'Yes, but I was nowhere *near* as big as she is!'

'I'm sure you were absolutely the right size,' Gabe said, kissing the top of her head.

'And are you and Warwick planning children or is that something I shouldn't ask?' Mia said.

'Mia!' Gabe cried. 'Give them a chance. They haven't even walked up the aisle yet.'

'Oh, Gabe! You're *so* old-fashioned. Life isn't all perfect and all in the correct order like a Jane Austen novel.'

'But Austen novel's *aren't* perfect. Think of

34

Willoughby and Colonel Brandon's ward, and what might have happened to Georgiana Darcy if wicked Wickham had had his way.'

Mia laughed. 'Don't you just *love* a man who knows his Austen?' she said, placing her arms around his waist and giving him a squeeze.

Katherine smiled and her gaze returned to the photograph of young Will and she couldn't help wondering if that's what the future held for her. She'd never thought that she was the kind to marry and have a family; her work had been her life up until this moment. Yet, here she was planning a wedding to the man she loved and who knew where that would lead her?

CHAPTER 6

Dan Harcourt had returned from a morning ride with Perseus and was just cleaning out the stables when a tall redhead entered the yard.

'Helloooo,' she cooed, peering into the dark depths of each stable in turn until she found Dan.

He stepped out into the sunshine, his red-gold hair catching the light. His skin was richly tanned and the checked sleeves of his shirt had been rolled up to reveal tanned arms that were now covered with a fine layer of dust.

'Good morning,' he said, looking at the stranger. She was wearing a pair of skin-tight navy jodhpurs and a white blouse that was open at the neck to reveal a very deep cleavage.

'I'm Carmel Hudson,' she said, extending a perfectly manicured hand. Dan shook it, surprised at the strength of her grip. 'You're going to be giving riding lessons, I understand,' she said.

'That's right,' Dan said with a smile. 'I'm hoping to take a few pupils from next month.'

'Good,' she said, 'because my little Charlotte wants some lessons. We've just bought her her first pony but I'm not the best teacher, I'm afraid.'

'How old is she?'

'Eight and very headstrong. Like her mother,' Carmel said with a little laugh that sounded like breaking glass. 'I'm afraid you won't find her an easy pupil. I'm *much* easier.'

Dan's eyes widened a fraction and he cleared his throat.

'And *I'd* like to book lessons too,' she added, looking him up and down.

'I'm not sure I could teach you anything, Mrs Hudson,' he said politely. 'I hear you're quite a horsewoman.'

'Please, call me Carmel,' she said, 'and I'm sure you could teach me an *awful* lot and I promise to be the best pupil ever.' She flashed him a coy smile.

'Well, we could book a preliminary lesson and see how we go from there,' he said. 'Why don't you give me a call in a couple of weeks? We're still setting things up here and we'll be more organised by then.'

'I'll do that,' she said, holding his gaze.

'Was there anything else, Mrs Hudson?'

'*Carmel!*' she said, her voice breathy with frustration. Dan nodded. 'And, yes, there was something else. We're at Hunter's Lodge – the converted barn on the road to Bewley Green. You know it?'

'I've ridden by a few times,' Dan said.

'Yes, I've seen you,' she said.

Dan swallowed hard.

'You'll have to come round for dinner some time,' she continued. 'My husband's away a lot and I get a bit ... bored. It'll be nice to have someone to talk to. About horses. I think we have a lot in common.'

'I'm afraid my evenings are rather busy with this place and my family, Mrs Hud-'

'*Carmel!*'

'Carmel,' he said. 'But I look forward to our first lesson.'

'Right,' she said, appraising him through half-closed eyes.

'So, give us a call, okay?' Dan said with a nod as he turned to disappear into one of the stables.

Carmel stood for a moment or two as if stunned

that he'd dismissed her thus and then strode out of the yard just as Robyn was entering it. Robyn watched in wide-eyed wonder as the red-head sashayed down the driveway.

'Dan?' she called, finding the stable he was mucking out.

'Hello,' he said. 'Where's Cassie?'

'Pammy's taken her down to the village hall for the coffee morning. 'She likes to show her off,' Robyn said. 'Who on *earth* was that woman?'

'Carmel Hudson,' Dan said, resting his weight against a broom for a moment. 'She wants lessons for her daughter. Charlotte.'

Robyn did a double-take. 'Oh, Dan!'

'What?'

'I've heard *dreadful* things about that child.'

'What dreadful things?'

'I was talking to Amy in the village. Her son started at the primary school this year and that girl made his life a misery. She's a dreadful bully!'

Dan laughed. 'Do I look as if I can't handle an eight-year old girl?'

'It's not just the girl I'm worried about,' Robyn said. 'What about her mother?'

'What about her?'

'Carmel Hudson is a *terrible* flirt.'

'How do you know?' he asked.

'How do I know? The whole village knows!'

'But you've never even met her,' Dan pointed out.

'I don't need to. Amy told me-'

Dan shook his head. 'You shouldn't listen to village gossip.'

'So, she *wasn't* flirting with you, then?' Robyn asked.

'I don't know,' Dan said, 'but I can assure you, *I* wasn't flirting with *her*.' He placed his dusty, tanned arms around Robyn's slim waist and kissed her on the tip of her nose. 'Carmel wants riding lessons too.'

'*She* wants lessons?' Robyn cried. 'But she's the best horsewoman in the whole of Hampshire! Or so I've heard,' she said with a little blush.

'We can all improve our technique,' Dan said.

'I don't think it's her riding technique she's interested in improving,' Robyn said.

Dan grinned and then slowly wiped one of his thumbs across Robyn's forehead.

'What are you doing?' she asked.

'Trying to iron out the frown that's sitting there.'

'Well, *you* put it there, Mr Harcourt!'

He looked into her eyes and shook his head. 'You're not jealous, are you?'

Robyn pouted. 'I just think you sometimes forget that you're a very handsome man and that women find you attractive.'

'I'm also a very happily married one,' he said and Robyn could protest no further because he kissed her.

CHAPTER 7

It was Thursday afternoon when Lily Lawton's silver
Audi pulled up at The Old Vicarage in a skidding halt
which Warwick heard from his study. He put his
fountain pen down carefully, making sure it didn't roll
off his desk into oblivion again, and walked across to
the large sash window. Dear Lily, he thought, here to
pour doom and gloom on the proceedings, no doubt.

His big sister was forty-four and a well-worn cynic
when it came to romantic relationships. He had
actually thought twice about inviting her to the
wedding but she was his only close relative and, cynic
or not, he couldn't bear the thought of her not being
there.

'*Married?*' she'd cried down the phone when he'd
told her the news. 'You're getting *married?* Whatever
for?' she'd said in the manner of Sir Walter Elliot in
the 1995 version of *Persuasion* when Captain
Wentworth declares his intentions towards Anne.

Warwick had tried to make her believe that he was
in love but his message hadn't seemed to get through.

Now, he left the comfort of his study to answer
the door, opening it to greet his sister who was
standing on the doorstep in an immaculate trouser
suit in steel-grey and a pair of enormous sunglasses
even though the sky was overcast.

'Lily!' he exclaimed, giving her a hug.

'Watch the hair, Warwick darling. I've just had it
done.'

'It looks marvellous,' he said, admiring the elfin cut
which showed off her sharp cheek bones. She looked
so like their mother, he thought, ushering her in.

'I've brought wine,' she said, taking a bottle of

white out of her enormous handbag. 'I don't know about you but this wedding makes *me* want to drink! I still don't know why you insist on marrying,' she said.

They walked through to the living room at the front of the house and sat down on a Knole sofa that virtually filled the space with its grandeur.

'Because, dear sister, I'm in love,' Warwick told her again with a happy sigh.

'You don't have to get married just because you're in love. Just have the occasional sleep over like I do. It's *much* easier!' she said, removing her sunglasses at last.

He laughed. 'I'm getting a bit too old for sleepovers,' he said, 'besides, I want to spend as much time with Katherine as I can and we can't do that with me here and her in Oxfordshire.'

Lily pursed her scarlet-lipsticked mouth at him. 'You mean, you're moving?'

Warwick nodded.

'You're selling The Old Vicarage?'

'Yep!'

'Oh, Warwick! When did this happen?' she asked as if he'd just told her that he'd committed some dreadful crime.

'We've decided that we want a new home together. Well, an *old* home. But a new start.'

'But you love this house!' Lily said.

'But I love Katherine more,' he said, a soppy smile on his face that he knew would wind Lily up. 'What can I say? We can find a wonderful place in Oxfordshire and make a new home there.'

'And why can't she move here? Why does it have to be you who moves?'

'Because her work's there. I can work anywhere.

It's all been discussed and I'm happy with the decision,' he said, his voice becoming firmer as if he was warning his sister that he wasn't going to brook any argument.

'She's got you wrapped around her little finger,' Lily said.

'Very likely.'

'I probably shouldn't say this,' Lily began and Warwick knew he was in for a tirade for, whenever Lily said *I probably shouldn't say this*, the listener was inevitably crushed by some tale of woe, 'but marriage is for foolish romantics who haven't grown up yet.'

'Then I should be absolutely fine,' Warwick said.

'Oh!' Lily cried. 'You're so infuriating! Open the wine!'

Warwick took the bottle of wine and left the room, returning a moment later with two full crystal-cut glasses. He watched as his sister kicked off her pair of expensive looking heels and curled her legs up underneath herself on the sofa.

'I don't mean to sound cynical,' Lily began, taking a modest sip of wine, 'but have you really thought about this. I mean *really* thought about it?'

Warwick sat back down next to her and smiled. 'Lily – I love you dearly but just because marriage didn't work out for you-'

'Twice!' she interrupted.

'Yes, twice, it doesn't mean it's not going to work for me. I'm truly sorry what happened with Jeff-'

'Cheating son of a-'

'And with Pete.'

'Paul,' Lily corrected.

Warwick nodded. His sister's marriage to Paul – after a whirlwind romance when she'd been working as a translator in Paris - hadn't even lasted a year and he had obviously put her off the institution of marriage for evermore. 'It's a great shame that you didn't find your own happy ending-'

Lily made a funny guttural noise that was part scoff, part grunt. 'Happy ending! There's no such thing outside one of your novels.'

Warwick shrugged. 'Well, I believe there is.'

'Do you? Do you really?' She cocked her head to one side and examined his face with intense closeness and he stared straight back at her. She managed to look both young and old at the same time as if the vulnerable little girl and the older cynic were still battling it out.

'I do,' he said.

'But to give up everything – your home, your bachelorhood-'

'I don't feel like I'm giving anything up. I'm simply moving forward,' he said, calmly sipping his wine.

'Oh, I give up on you!' Lily said at last. 'You've lost your mind.'

'No, dear sister,' Warwick said. 'I've lost my heart.'

That night, before bed, Warwick took down the old black and white photograph of his mother, Lara Lawton, that lived on the mahogany chest of drawers in his bedroom. It had been taken when she was in her twenties and she looked like a Hollywood starlet. She'd been desperate to make a career as an actress but had never graduated beyond bit parts and, when she'd had Lily and Warwick, she'd settled for the more modest role of secretary. But she'd always been a romantic and had passed those genes on to Warwick rather than his sister.

'Believe in love and it will come your way,' she'd told him and he'd believed her only it had taken its time. He'd known it when it had arrived, though. He'd known it with Katherine's very first letter to him even though she'd thought she'd been writing to a woman. He'd adored her openness and her passion for the written word and they'd become the very best of friends even before they'd met.

'You'd have loved her,' he told the photograph of his mother, and a great weight of sadness filled his heart that she wasn't alive to see him get married. His father had died when he'd been very young and he couldn't really remember much about him but he felt the loss of his mother still and was quite sure that she would have loved Katherine.

'I'm doing the right thing, aren't I?' he said to the photograph. 'Lily's got it all wrong, hasn't she?'

The face of his mother stared back at him softly, gently and silently.

CHAPTER 8

It was Thursday afternoon – the day before Katherine and Warwick were due to meet at Purley Hall. They'd arranged to arrive at lunchtime on Friday which would give them plenty to time to make sure that everything was in place for the big day on Saturday. Dame Pamela had also invited them to dinner in the evening along with Robyn and Dan – their maid of honour and best man – although Katherine felt quite sure that she wouldn't be able to eat a single morsel.

Being super-organised, she was just about packed. There was just one special item that had yet to be wrapped – the wedding dress. It was laid out upon her toile de jouy bedding and Katherine gazed down at it through tear-misted eyes. She had never seen anything so beautiful. Well, not since Matthew Macfadyen had strode across the dawn meadow in the 2005 adaptation of *Pride and Prejudice*. She really didn't feel worthy of such a dress and it felt like a terrible extravagance to have something so lovely for just one day.

But that's what being a bride is all about, a little voice inside her said. *Every woman is entitled to one perfect day when she is the star attraction.*

So why did she feel so guilty? Her life, up until now, had been so simple and so modest. Her work outfits were conservatively cut in muted colours. There was never anything that drew too much attention to herself because that wasn't the sort of person she was. Of course, it was wonderful to get dressed up every now and again like at the Jane Austen conferences at Purley Hall. Then, a different Katherine would emerge like a resplendent butterfly, glorifying in fabulous fabrics in rich colours.

It was hard to imagine herself as a bride. Shelley had done the most marvellous job with the dress and Katherine could never have imagined it would be so beautiful but she still couldn't quite envisage herself on the day.

Uncle Ned would be there to give her away because her father had left home when Katherine was just seven. Her mother had died a few years ago but her mother's brother, Katherine's Uncle Ned, was still around. He lived in York and had just retired from teaching and had been delighted to get Katherine's call.

'In costume, you say?' he'd said with a laugh.

Katherine had been worried that she'd put him off but he accepted with alacrity.

Katherine would also have her best friend, Chrissie, at the wedding. Chrissie Carter was her jogging partner. One summer morning six years ago, they'd met at a stile whilst out jogging and they'd been pounding the Oxfordshire countryside together ever since. Katherine adored her friend and the two of them had enjoyed many a jog whilst setting the world to rights which usually involved complaining about the dearth of men. Well, until Katherine and Warwick had become an item.

'Oh, you're so lucky, Katherine!' Chrissie had said when she'd seen the Georgian ring sparkling on her finger. 'I'm convinced I'm going to remain an old maid.'

Katherine shook her head. 'You know what Jane Austen said?'

'No, but I'm *sure* you're going to tell me.'

'Do not be in a hurry: depend upon it, the right man will

come at last.'

'She really said that?'

'Amongst other glorious things, yes,' Katherine said. 'Let me lend you some of her novels some time.'

'Oh, no!' Chrissie had said. 'I'm not wading through pages and pages of dance scenes and proposals but I might borrow the Colin Firth adaptation from you again.'

Katherine smiled at the memory. She was thrilled that Chrissie was coming to the wedding. She would be a joyous presence and Katherine couldn't wait to see what she would wear. Although her dear friend wasn't a fellow Janeite, she had agreed to dress in Regency costume on the day and had booked one of Dame Pamela's outfits.

Leaving the bedroom, Katherine went downstairs. Her two cats, Freddie and Fitz, were to be delivered to a neighbour that evening and were currently curled up together on top of a favourite blanket on a balloon back chair in the kitchen.

This is the last time I'll be in my little home as a single lady, she thought to herself. How strange that felt. When she next returned, it would be as a married woman although, in all likelihood, Warwick wouldn't be with her. They wouldn't be together properly as husband and wife until they'd found a new home.

Suddenly, her heart flipped at the thought of the Katherine in the future. Wife, partner, co-habiter and, catching sight of her reflection in the kitchen window, she wondered if she was really up to the job.

Great grey rain clouds filled the sky and the air was warm and muggy when Higgins entered Dame Pamela's room early on Friday morning and opened the curtains.

'Good morning, madam,' he said, placing a cup of tea on her bedside table.

'But it's still dark,' she said.

'Rain has been forecast,' Higgins said. 'Rain followed by a stiff breeze and intermittent showers.'

Dame Pamela grimaced. 'And tomorrow?'

'Unsettled.'

'Oh, dear!'

'With a chance of sunshine.'

Dame Pamela sat up in bed, pushing her long, white hair over her shoulders. Higgins was the only person on the planet who saw Dame Pamela before she got to work with the hairbrush, make-up and diamonds. She took a sip of her tea from her bone china mug covered in pretty violets which was used every morning and then she swung her legs out of bed, her feet finding her cerise sequinned slippers.

'Do you know, Higgins, I actually have butterflies in my stomach. Isn't that funny? I haven't had butterflies since I received that *Cream of the Screen* award and was kissed by Daniel Craig when he presented it to me!'

'Indeed, madam,' Higgins said.

'Nothing beats a wedding, does it?' she said, her eyes suddenly dreamy. 'What was that lovely line from *Mansfield Park*? "I would have everybody marry if they can do it properly". That was it, wasn't it?'

'Very likely, madam,' Higgins said.

'And Warwick and Katherine are certainly doing it properly,' she said, walking across to her dressing table and picking up the hairbrush. 'I feel so honoured that they chose Purley Hall. We must have more weddings here in the future, Higgins. I can't think of anything I'd like more. And Austen-themed weddings at that.'

'Yes, madam,' Higgins said.

Later that morning, once Dame Pamela had coiffed her hair and had dressed in a pale mint-coloured dress accessorised with a very modest single string of pearls, she went outside to check on the proceedings.

The white marquee stood on the lawn by the lake. The tables and chairs and all the necessary crockery would arrive later that day. There was a lot to see to but Robyn was on hand to liaise with the wedding planner and everything, it seemed, was under control.

Walking along the banks of the little river that ran through the grounds of Purley, Dame Pamela couldn't help thinking about her own weddings of the past and the sense of anticipation and joy that filled the days before. Were Katherine and Warwick feeling like that now, she wondered? And would Dame Pamela ever have those feelings again?

She sighed, looking back at the great Georgian house whose windows winked at her in the morning light. It was hard to imagine sharing her life with somebody now but Dame Pamela believed that one should never say never and, of course, she was a die-hard romantic and that meant that life was always full of possibilities.

CHAPTER 9

The drive from The Old Vicarage in West Sussex to Purley Hall in Hampshire was not a long one but, when a cynical sister was sitting beside you, the miles seemed to stretch to infinity.

At Midhurst, Lily was recounting the time that she'd caught Jeff in a clinch with their neighbour.

'He didn't even try to deny it,' she said, as if still surprised. 'He just sort of shrugged as if it was to be expected.'

And, by Petersfield, she'd moved on to the misdemeanours of Paul who had emptied their joint bank account and gambled the lot at online casinos. 'I tried to help him. I tried to understand but he didn't want to be helped.'

'I'm so sorry, Lily,' Warwick said.

'But this is what I'm trying to tell you – you can never truly know a person. I don't think human beings are meant to live together.'

'Oh, you can't be serious!' Warwick said with a laugh as he slowed to take a bend in the road.

'I'm dead serious,' Lily said, her mouth a thin, straight line of intense seriousness. 'At least, I don't think men and women should live together.'

'What are you saying?' Warwick asked, casting a quick glance her way. 'You're not-'

'No!' she cried. 'But I'm never *ever* living with another man again.'

They drove on in silence, finally turning off the main roads and slowing down to take the winding country lanes of Hampshire.

'I just think,' Lily started up again, 'that you're absolutely mad to be going through all this when you don't need to. In this day and age, you don't need to get married.'

'I know,' Warwick said.

'Society couldn't care less. Marriage is outdated and old-fashioned.'

'But you believed in it once. *Twice!*'

'Yes, well, I'm over that now and I can pass on my great wisdom to you,' she said.

Warwick shook his head. 'But I don't need your wisdom. Every person has to make their own decisions in life. It's virtually impossible to learn from somebody else's mistakes; there are too many variables.'

'Oh, I give up!' Lily said and Warwick laughed.

'You're acting like I'm going to my execution rather than my wedding,' he said.

'And so you are, dear brother. And so you are!'

Katherine's taxi pulled up at the front of Horseshoe Cottage just before one in the afternoon and, for a moment, she didn't move. The taxi driver turned around.

'This is the right place, isn't it?' he said, a puzzled expression on his face.

'Oh, yes,' Katherine said, reaching for her purse.

'You okay? You look like you've seen a ghost. Not haunted, is it, this old cottage?'

She shook her head and paid him. 'No,' she said.

Robyn, who'd been sitting in the kitchen at the front of the house, eagerly awaiting her guest, leapt to her feet and rushed to the door, flinging it open and running down the garden path.

'Katherine!' she screamed, pulling her into an embrace. 'Oh, I'm so excited, I can barely breathe!'

'And I won't be able to either if you don't loosen your grip!'

Robyn laughed. 'Let me help you with your things. Oh!' she cried, spying the wedding dress on the back seat.

Katherine opened the taxi door and carefully took the dress out in its protective wrapping.

'I'll get your suitcase,' Robyn said and the two of them headed into the cottage.

Katherine smiled as she took in Horseshoe Cottage. It looked just as she'd imagined it would. The living room housed a squashy sofa covered in tapestry cushions and two armchairs covered in books, newspapers and a couple of half-eaten dog biscuits.

'Take a seat in the kitchen and I'll make us a cup of tea,' Robyn said. 'I'll just take your things upstairs.'

The kitchen was tiny but homely with a small square pine table in the middle of the room and a dresser at the back full of pretty crockery. There was a shiny blue Aga from which hung a polka-dotted tea towel, a baby's bonnet and a pair of walking socks, and, on the worktop next to the dresser was an egg skelter filled with brown and white eggs, some of which were covered in straw and feathers.

Katherine walked over to the dresser and picked up a photo frame and saw the smiling, shining faces of Robyn and Dan. They were outside the Jane Austen House Museum in Chawton and had their arms around each other. Robyn looked inexplicably happy. She had, at last, found a man she could share her love of Jane Austen with. Katherine smiled and replaced the photo frame.

'I've shut the dogs in the utility room so you don't

need to worry about paw prints on your dress,' Robyn said as she entered the kitchen and Katherine was reminded of the exuberant Bingley in Bath. 'And Cassie is with Dan and Pammy up at the hall so it's just you and me.'

'Is Warwick here yet?'

'I don't think so,' Robyn said. 'Dan would have rung. He's up at the house waiting for him. He's arriving with his sister.'

Katherine nodded. 'Lily,' she said. 'She's staying in the pub in the village.'

'What's she like?' Robyn asked, pulling out a chair at the table for Katherine whilst she put the kettle on one of the Aga's hotplates to boil. 'I can't wait to meet her.'

'She's an acquired taste,' Katherine said with a wry smile.

'Oh?'

'She's not like us,' Katherine went on. 'She hates novels and doesn't believe in happy endings in life *or* in fiction.'

Robyn's mouth gaped open in horror. 'Hates novels? But novels are *life*!'

Katherine nodded. 'I'm afraid it's a hopeless case when it comes to Lily. Warwick's not given up on her, of course, and posts her a copy of each novel he writes but I don't think she ever reads them.'

Robyn's face was full of anguish at such a declaration. 'But to live in a world without novels-'

'I know!'

'And without believing in a happy ending!'

'It's unthinkable, isn't it?' Katherine said.

'Has she tried Jane Austen?'

'Warwick's tried to convert her *so* many times. He

bought her a box set of adaptations one Christmas but she posted them back to him with "Don't do that again" written on a scrap of paper.'

'Shocking!' Robyn said, taking the kettle off the hotplate and making tea in two white mugs on which were written quotes from *Pride and Prejudice*. Robyn took the one which read, "In vain have I struggled" and gave Katherine the one which read, "How shall I bear such happiness!'

Placing a Regency-style sugar bowl and milk jug on the table, Robyn sat down next to Katherine.

'It's all Warwick could do to get Lily to come to the wedding,' Katherine went on. 'She's been married and divorced twice and is quite opposed to weddings. In fact, she's probably bending his ear about all that right now.'

'Poor Warwick,' Robyn said. 'Maybe you'll be able to convert her once you're sisters-in-law.'

'Well, miracles do happen,' Katherine said.

Robyn nodded. 'If there's one thing Jane Austen has taught me it's to believe in happy endings. I can't bear the thought of somebody out there not having that optimism to lift their spirits.'

'I know,' Katherine said.

'Anyway,' Robyn said, 'how are *you?*'

'I'm fine,' Katherine said, taking a sip of her tea.

'Are you sure?' Robyn asked, her head cocked to one side. 'Because it isn't long ago since my own wedding and I'll never forget those nerves!'

'You were nervous?' Katherine asked in surprise.

'Of *course!*' Robyn said with a laugh. 'Nervous that everything would go okay and that I wouldn't fluff my lines. Nervous that Dan would turn up and not suddenly realise that he'd made a big mistake.

Nervous that Jace might gallop up the aisle on a horse and disrupt everything! I think I was nervous in every way imaginable!'

'But not nervous that you were making a mistake?' Katherine said in a voice barely above a whisper.

Robyn shook her head. 'No. I don't think I was ever nervous about that.'

'But how did you know – I mean, *really* know, that you were making the right decision?'

Robyn sat perfectly still for a moment, gazing into the middle distance. 'I just knew,' she said and then she caught Katherine's gaze. 'I'm sorry if that's not very helpful but it was such a strong feeling that it completely vanquished the nerves in the end.'

Katherine smiled.

'Katherine,' Robyn began, 'you're not having second thoughts, are you?'

Katherine didn't answer at first. She was staring into the sugar bowl as if it was the most important thing in the world. 'No,' she said at last. 'Of course not.'

Robyn smiled and rested her hand on hers. 'Good,' she said. 'I've never known a couple more suited than you and Warwick.'

'Really?'

'Really,' Robyn said. 'Why? Don't *you* think you're suited?'

'Well, we're just so different,' she said. 'Warwick's so enthusiastic and demonstrative and I'm so – so –'

'But you're the same too,' Robyn interrupted. 'Your love of Jane Austen and books and writing and architecture.'

'Yes,' Katherine said and they smiled at each other.

'Now,' Robyn said. 'Why don't you go and settle in

upstairs? Take a shower or go for a walk whilst I prepare lunch. There are some chairs out in the garden too if you just fancy sitting quietly. My favourite spot is under the apple tree near the hen run.'

Katherine nodded. At that moment in her life, it sounded like the most perfect place in the world.

It was Dan who answered the door to Warwick and Lily.

'Warwick!' he said, clapping him on the back and ushering him inside. 'And you must be Lily.'

Lily looked up at the tall, handsome man who was smiling like an Adonis and couldn't help blushing. 'Yes,' she said, shaking his hand.

Warwick smiled. Even Lily wasn't immune to the charms of Dan Harcourt.

'Pammy's upstairs with Cassandra,' Dan said. 'We're to have a spot of lunch in the kitchen. Higgins has it all prepared and then the afternoon is yours to settle in and relax.'

Lily made a funny guttural noise and Dan turned, blinking in surprise.

'Everything okay?' he asked.

'Relax!' Lily scoffed. 'How can I possibly relax when my brother's about to-'

'Become happily married,' Warwick interrupted, taking her hand and patting it gently but firmly.

Dan looked at the pair quizzically but was too polite to ask what was going on. 'So,' he said at last, 'let's eat, shall we?'

CHAPTER 10

After a delicious ham salad with fresh baguette and a generous slice of Victoria Sandwich washed down with several cups of tea, Warwick drove Lily into the village so she could book into her room at the pub.

'That Dan's rather attractive,' she said as Warwick helped her with her bags into her room.

'And very married,' Warwick said.

'I didn't say I was interested,' Lily said, flicking her short dark hair in annoyance. 'I was merely making an observation.'

Warwick smiled. 'My dear sister, you will never be immune to the charms of the opposite sex no matter how much you protest to hate men.'

'I never said I've sworn right off men,' Lily said, 'merely marrying the brutes!' She flopped down on the bed and kicked off her heels.

'Will you be okay here?' Warwick asked. 'You're sure you don't want to join us at the hall for dinner later?'

Lily shook her head. 'You go back and enjoy your last night of freedom as a bachelor,' she said, 'unless you finally see sense and do a runner, that is.'

'I'm not going to do a runner,' he said.

'Yes, well, there's plenty of time to make your mind up yet.'

Warwick shook his head in despair at Lily and bent to kiss her cheek. 'I'll see you tomorrow,' he told her. 'I'll be the one standing at the top of the aisle, waiting for my bride and *not* doing a runner.'

'We'll see,' Lily said.

It was seven thirty that evening when Katherine

and Robyn walked up the driveway to join everyone at Purley Hall. The afternoon had passed by in a blur of reading, chatting, drinking tea and walking through the village and Katherine now felt a little more relaxed than when she'd first arrived thanks to Robyn's hospitality and sweetness.

Higgins answered the door, looking resplendent in a shiny green waistcoat covered in gold fleur de lys.

'Dr Roberts, welcome,' he said, taking her jacket.

'Good evening, Higgins,' Katherine said, happy to see her favourite butler again.

'Hello, Higgins,' Robyn said. 'How's Cassie?'

But Higgins didn't get a chance to reply because it was then that Dan walked into the hallway from the drawing room with a sleeping Cassandra in his arms.

'She's getting heavy,' Dan said, bending to kiss Robyn.

Robyn stroked her daughter's golden curls. 'I hope she's been a good girl for her Aunt Pammy?'

'Certainly has,' Dan said, just as his phone vibrated in his pocket. 'Here,' he said, passing Cassandra to Robyn.

'My, she's grown,' Katherine said, stepping forward to admire the sleeping girl as she settled into Robyn's arms.

'Oh, yes!' Robyn said, pride dancing in her eyes. 'She'll be dressing up and taking part in our Austen weekends before you know it.' She looked up as Dan popped his phone in his pocket again. 'Who was that?'

'Oh, nothing important,' he said but there was a look of anxiety in his eyes. 'Hello, Katherine.' He leant forward to kiss her. 'How are you?'

'Very well,' she said.

'All ready for the big day?'

'Well, I-'

Just then, Warwick emerged from the drawing room and, striding across the hallway, took Katherine in his arms and kissed her passionately.

Dame Pamela, who had followed him, laughed. 'Save it for the wedding night!' she cried and the five of them went into dinner together.

As usual, dinner at Purley was a treat and they all enjoyed a perfect summer menu of watercress soup, an asparagus risotto and the lightest of lemon sorbets for dessert.

'That was absolutely delicious, Dame Pamela,' Warwick said, dabbing his mouth with a white linen napkin once the meal was finished.

'But it will be nothing compared to tomorrow's fare,' Dame Pamela said. 'Your menu looks absolutely divine!'

'And all Austen-inspired,' Warwick said.

'Like everything else!' Robyn said.

'Naturally,' Dame Pamela said. 'I really don't see how anyone can choose anything else when it comes to a wedding. I mean, all these horrendous Disney-themed weddings or people dressing up as characters from *Alice in Wonderland*. It's absolutely awful!'

'Each to their own, I suppose,' Warwick said.

'Yes but nothing can top Jane Austen. She encapsulates the very essence of Englishness with the elegance of the dress, the sobriety of the language and the perfection of the manners.'

'You sound like you're reading from a script again, Pammy,' Dan said and then his phone vibrated again. 'Sorry,' he said. 'I'll switch it off.' Robyn caught his eye as if to say, *what's going on* but he cleared his throat and changed the subject. 'So, will it be sunny skies tomorrow?' he asked.

'I have every faith in the weather,' Dame Pamela said. 'The stormy sky and rain was today and, no matter what the weathermen say, the sun *will* come out tomorrow. And, no, I'm not about to break into song.'

Robyn giggled. She was quite used to Dame Pamela's occasional bursts into song in the office. Just a couple of days ago, her boss had worked her way through a medley from *Cats*, *Evita* and *Sunset Boulevard*. It always made Robyn smile although she had yet to pluck up the courage to join in herself.

'So,' Dame Pamela continued, 'what an inspired idea to have your wedding in the year when we are celebrating the two hundredth birthday of *Pride and Prejudice*.'

'Well, we couldn't think of anything more romantic, could we, Katherine?' Warwick said.

'That's right,' she replied.

'Every true Janeite will be celebrating this year and what better way to do that than by marrying your true love?' Warwick said, his dark eyes sparkling in the candlelight.

'Oh, how romantic!' Dame Pamela said, clasping her hands to her chest.

'Can you believe *Pride and Prejudice* is two hundred years old?' Robyn said.

'Mr Darcy is doing very well for his age,' Dame Pamela said with a little chuckle. 'Pleasing women for two centuries is no mean feat!'

Everybody laughed and Warwick proposed a toast. 'Happy Birthday, Mr Darcy!' he said and they all echoed his sentiments, clinking their glasses with each other as they did so.

'Pammy – tell them about the mad American,' Dan said.

Everybody fixed eager eyes on Dame Pamela.

'Ah, yes!' she said, drawing in a great breath as if she was about to give a great performance – which she probably was. 'I had a telephone call from this American businessman. He'd heard about my first edition copy of *Pride and Prejudice* and wanted to make me an offer for it.' She paused, glancing at her rapt audience around the table. 'He offered me a million dollars.'

Katherine gasped. 'You didn't sell it, did you?'

Dame Pamela looked shocked. 'Of course not! And I told him that I wouldn't sell it even if he offered me ten million dollars.'

'And what did he say?' Warwick asked.

'He said he wasn't offering ten million dollars but he would go to five million.'

Warwick's mouth dropped open and Katherine gave a nervous sort of laugh. 'And you still refused?' she said.

'I most certainly did and I jolly well told him to go and find himself a first edition of *The Great Gatsby* or something American because *Pride and Prejudice* was *not* leaving England!'

Everybody applauded Dame Pamela and she blushed with pride.

'Quite right, Dame Pamela, quite right!' Warwick said.

'Money can't buy *every*thing, you know,' she said. 'There are some things in this life that are priceless.'

Warwick caught Katherine's eyes and winked at her.

Coffee and biscuits were served in the drawing room as the last light faded from the western sky in a show of violet and rose, and conversation moved easily from subject to subject until the lantern clock on the sideboard chimed ten o'clock and Katherine sprang to her feet.

'Goodness! How late it is,' she said. 'Dame Pamela – thank you so much for a lovely dinner.'

'It was my pleasure,' she said, standing up and embracing her guest. 'Have a good night's sleep, my darling.' She kissed Katherine on both cheeks, her diamond drop earrings swinging like pendulums.

'Goodnight, everyone,' Robyn said, standing up.

'Do you want an escort?' Dan asked.

'No, we'll be fine. My eyes have finally adjusted to life in the country,' she told Katherine. 'There are no street lights between here and our cottage but there is a bit of a moon around so we should be okay.'

The men, who were staying at the hall, escorted the ladies to the front door.

'Dan, who was that on the phone during dinner?' Robyn asked.

'It was nobody,' he said rather unconvincingly.

'Well, it must have been something important for them to keep ringing you over and over like that.'

'It wasn't anything to worry about.'

Robyn's face fell into an expression that clearly said she *was* worried. 'And you'll be all right with Cassie?' she asked, having already checked on her daughter several times since dinner.

'Of course,' he said, 'and I know where you are if we need anything!'

She smiled. 'It's going to be funny not having you both at the cottage.'

'It's just for one night,' he said.

'I know.'

They kissed and said goodnight and then it was Katherine and Warwick's turn. They were standing a little apart from Robyn and Dan and their foreheads were pressed together.

'Feels strange, doesn't it?' Warwick said to Katherine, taking her hand and squeezing it.

She nodded. 'Yes.'

'The next time we see each other, it'll be to say "I do".'

Katherine took a deep breath and sighed it out slowly. 'Yes,' she said again.

Warwick leaned back and tipped his head to one side. 'You okay? You were very quiet at dinner.'

'I was just thinking,' she told him.

'We'd better get going,' Robyn said, 'before those great clouds hide the moon.'

Warwick bent forward and kissed Katherine. 'I love you, Miss Roberts.'

'*Dr* Roberts!' she said with a little smile.

'I love her too,' Warwick said and they kissed again.

Katherine and Robyn then left the hall and walked down the driveway. It had turned into a world of silhouettes and shadows and the air was soft and cool. The moon was bright and guided them back to Horseshoe Cottage and a tawny owl provided a haunting soundtrack as they walked.

Katherine went straight up to the guest bedroom.

'I'm sorry it's so small,' Robyn said as she stood in the doorway to say goodnight. There was a pretty single bed with an ornate white metal frame, a bedside chair and a tiny dressing table on which had been placed a sea-green jug filled with white roses.

'It's perfect,' Katherine said.

'Do you have everything you need?'

'I think so.'

'Well, I'm just next door if you do need anything,' Robyn told her.

'Thank you,' Katherine said. 'It's so kind of you to let me stay.'

'It's my pleasure. I'm so excited about tomorrow.'

'Are you getting up early?' Katherine asked.

'I usually do but only since having Cassandra. My sleep is all over the place these days but please don't feel that you have to get up at the crack of dawn. Just take your time. The carriage isn't arriving until quarter to four.'

'Now, *there's* a sentence a girl doesn't hear every day,' Katherine said with a grin.

Robyn laughed. 'You're going to feel like Cinderella!'

'I hope not. I much prefer Jane Austen's heroines to those insipid ones in fairy tales,' Katherine said.

'You're going to look perfect, I just know it!' Robyn said. 'You'll be Elizabeth Bennet and Cinderella all rolled into one!'

Katherine couldn't help but laugh at that.

'Good night,' Robyn said with a smile before shutting the door.

Katherine closed her eyes for a moment, savouring the peace. When would she next have a quiet moment to herself, she wondered? Tomorrow would be one big whirl of activity and noise. What was that lovely bit she adored so much in *Northanger Abbey* when poor Catherine Morland is finding the Upper Rooms in Bath so daunting?

'I think we had better sit still, for one gets so tumbled in such a crowd!'

Katherine smiled as she remembered it. Was that what it was going to be like tomorrow? Would she and Warwick be pushed and tumbled and not find a moment to be still – to be alone?

Katherine sighed. She had unpacked her things that afternoon and now set her little travel clock on the bedside chair next to her trusty travelling copy of *Pride and Prejudice*. She would treat herself to a few chapters before she went to sleep.

CHAPTER 11

Saturday morning dawned bright and clear. For half an hour, Katherine lay awake in bed listening to the rich clear notes of a blackbird in an apple tree before drifting back to sleep in the knowledge that it wasn't going to rain on her wedding day and all would be well. But, unseen, the clouds were gathering over the wild stretches of the New Forest and it seemed that they had one direction in mind – Purley Hall.

By mid-morning, the first fat raindrops were falling, pit-pattering on rooftops and sliding down windowpanes. The florist had arrived with a team of helpers who were busy decorating the hall and the library where the ceremony was going to take place as well as the marquee and the temple on the island, dodging the showers as best as they could. Dame Pamela was flitting around, casting her eyes to the lavender-coloured sky and shaking her head in dismay at the pearly curtain of rain.

'This is not what we ordered, Higgins,' she said to the butler who was in the library where the chairs were being set out for the wedding ceremony.

'No, madam,' he said.

'I only hope the sun makes an appearance before the bride does.'

Horseshoe Cottage was a blessed haven away from the madness of the wedding preparations and Katherine was so grateful to Robyn for suggesting that she stayed there but she wasn't so happy when she saw the rain.

'Just look at that sky!' she said, peering out of the kitchen window and grimacing. 'It's not going to clear in time, is it?'

'Oh, I think it will,' Robyn said. 'I think those clouds are on their way north and will be chased away by sunshine long before the ceremony begins, leaving everything freshly washed and smelling delicious.'

'Do you?' Katherine asked.

Robyn nodded. 'I do.'

'I wish I had your optimism,' Katherine said.

They were sitting in the kitchen and were glad of the cheering warmth of the Aga even though it was July. Robyn had made scrambled eggs on wholemeal toast for breakfast and Katherine was now sipping an orange juice.

'Robyn, when you first moved in with Dan, what was it like?'

'Cramped,' Robyn said with a smile. 'We had so many boxes between us, we couldn't move for weeks!'

'No, I mean-'

'What was it *really* like?' Robyn said with a knowing expression on her face.

Katherine nodded.

'Well, after Jace, I knew that anything – any*one* - would be a breeze.'

Katherine nodded again, remembering the errant ex-boyfriend who had terrorised Robyn at a previous conference at Purley.

'And you were happy? You didn't feel like...' her voice faded away, her sentence unfinished.

'Like what?'

'Like you'd become less of yourself.'

Robyn frowned as if she didn't quite understand what Katherine meant.

'I don't think so,' she said, and she bit her lip as if

in deep thought. 'I remember feeling this wonderful peace – as if something in me had settled. That sounds funny, doesn't it? As if I started to wear big furry slippers and stop worrying about what I looked like. But it wasn't that. It was more that I felt content – a real feeling of contentedness.' She smiled. 'Does that make sense?'

Katherine nodded.

'And Dan was so sweet. He made such an effort to make me feel at home here. He made me a new run for my hens, let me pile all my cushions on the sofa and even let me keep my pink chintz bedding. And he genuinely seems to enjoy the occasional Jane Austen adaptation but he did fall asleep towards the end of the recent *Mansfield Park*,' Robyn said with a wry grin.

'Ah,' Katherine said, 'an adaptation too far. You should have stuck with *Pride and Prejudice* and *Sense and Sensibility*. It's a rare man that can stomach anything more than that.'

'But you haven't got to worry about that with Warwick,' Robyn said.

Katherine nodded. 'True but I sometimes worry that we're too alike in that respect.'

'What do you mean?' Robyn asked.

'I'm scared that we're going to turn into each other or morph together like those dreadful married couples you sometimes see who wear the same clothes and have the same haircuts.'

Robyn laughed. 'You won't be like that!'

'I just worry that I'm going to wake up in a year's time and not recognise myself anymore.'

'But life changes all of us – you don't have to get married for that. It wasn't long ago that I was doing a job I hated in a college in the Yorkshire Dales and living with someone who made me miserable and now look at me!'

'Life moves at an alarming pace sometimes,' Katherine said.

'But it's only alarming if you're going in a direction you don't want to be going in, isn't it?'

Katherine didn't answer. She was gazing down at her engagement ring and her face had turned marble-white.

The telephone in the hallway rang before Robyn had a chance to ask if Katherine was okay and she went through to answer it.

'Hello?' she said. There was a pause at the other end of the line and Robyn heard somebody hang up. She sighed and walked back through to the kitchen. 'That's odd,' she said. 'That's the second time that's happened this morning.'

Warwick had woken up just before the weather had turned and had gone out running. It was something he'd been doing a lot recently because he wanted to look his best. He'd used to run all the time but had somehow got out of the habit, preferring his rock climbing expeditions to the Peak District and Lake District but those trips were difficult to fit in with his writing commitments and he'd felt like he was getting out of shape.

That was one of the downsides of being a writer – it was so easy to spend the whole day indoors, glued to a computer screen and getting no exercise whatsoever. He'd just signed another three book deal with his publisher, Parnaby and Fox, who published a hardback in time for the Christmas market and the paperback in time to catch the summer sales and, once again, Nadia had negotiated him a pretty good deal. He had to be the best paid man writing as a woman in the whole of the UK, he thought, but the next deadline was tighter than usual and he'd been working longer hours because of it.

Now, back from his run and breakfasted courtesy of Higgins who had brought a silver tray into his room so loaded with good food that Warwick had felt certain that the poor butler was about to topple over, he sat himself down at the mahogany dressing table by the window and started writing.

He wasn't sure how much time had passed when a soft knock on the door brought him out of his writing trance.

'Come in.'

'Morning, Warwick,' Dan said. 'Not disturbing you, I hope?'

'No, no!' Warwick said, pushing his notepad away from him and giving Dan his full attention.

'Don't worry, I'm not wearing this to the wedding,' Dan said, motioning to his black T-shirt and blue jeans.

'It's a bit early to change, isn't it?' Warwick said.

'A few hours yet,' Dan nodded.

'Thought I'd get some writing in.'

'Really?' Dan said in surprise. 'You can do that on a day like today?'

'It's funny but days like today are often when I can write my best.'

'Wow,' Dan said. 'I couldn't do a thing on our wedding day except pace up and down and take Biscuit for half a dozen walks.'

Warwick grinned. 'Plus I've got this crazy deadline to meet.'

'Ah,' Dan said and then he frowned. 'You're not going to be writing on your honeymoon, are you?'

Warwick laughed. 'Probably! But that's okay, Katherine will most likely want to get some work in too.'

Dan shook his head. 'I'm glad I'm not an arty type like you guys. It must be impossible to switch off.'

'Pretty much,' Warwick said. 'But that's part of the fun too – you see inspiration everywhere you go. The only problem is finding time to capture it all.'

Dame Pamela had hired a team of hairdressers and beauticians to take care of Katherine, Robyn and herself and they were busy at work at Horseshoe Cottage. Katherine's hair had been washed and blow-dried and a girl was now working her magic with the hot wand, making her long dark locks look smooth and shiny. Both she and Robyn were wearing their hair loose with white ribbons and rosebuds threaded through.

The bride and her maid of honour had already had their hands massaged with almond oil, their nails had been shaped and painted with clear varnish and there was somebody now at work on their feet and toes.

'This feels wonderfully decadent,' Robyn said. 'I'd forgotten what it feels like to be pampered like this. I guess motherhood focuses the attention away from oneself.'

'So, who's looking after Cassandra today?'

'There's a lovely lady from the next village who's a childminder. She's taken Cassie along to her home today. She's got a little girl of her own called Belle and Cassie and Belle adore each other.'

'Are you missing her?' Katherine dared to ask.

'Like crazy!' Robyn said. 'But I have to admit that this is rather nice.'

Katherine smiled at the sight of her maid of honour who had her right foot in the pedicurist's hand whilst her long blonde hair was being brushed by somebody else.

'I wonder how the men are getting on,' Robyn said. 'Do you think they're dressed by now?'

'If I know Warwick, he'll probably leave it until the very last minute,' Katherine said.

The clock in the hallway at Purley slowly ticked the minutes away. The florists were misting the floral displays with water. Two huge urns filled with stargazer lilies had been placed in the library at the top of the aisle and pink and white roses tumbled and spilled from vases on the mantelpiece and windowsills.

The marquee was filled with flowers too and tall white candle displays surrounded by roses had been placed at the centre of each table. Silver and glass sparkled against the white tablecloths and blue and white ribbons and balloons hung above the area where the bride and groom and guests would dance later that evening.

Dame Pamela was thrilled with the results, Higgins had nodded his approval and Dan had smiled in wonder when he'd seen it all. The only person not to have taken any interest thus far was the groom who still hadn't made an appearance.

CHAPTER 12

It was three o'clock on Saturday afternoon when Doris Norris walked out of Winchester train station and looked around anxiously. She'd travelled from the Cotswolds and was meant to be meeting someone and couldn't help feeling a mite nervous at the prospect. What would everyone at Purley Hall say? Doris had told Robyn, of course, and the sweet girl had said it was absolutely fine and had told Doris not to worry but she couldn't help worrying all the same.

She tutted to herself as she remembered the events that had led to her current predicament. She'd just taken a walk into the village to pick up her copy of *Crochet Today* and to treat herself to a bag of mint toffees when a booming voice sounded from the door of the little shop.

'Don't just stand in the doorway like that! I can't get through!'

Doris would have recognised that voice anywhere and turned to see the bulky figure of Mrs Soames filling the shop doorway and startling the locals.

Mrs Soames in *her* village! It had been something of a shock at first but she'd soon been informed that Mrs Soames's daughter lived in the village and that she was visiting because, in Mrs Soames's words, she'd "gone and lost her job."

'Silly girl!' Mrs Soames had declared, shaking her head so that her chins had wobbled most alarmingly. 'As though jobs grow on trees these days! What *was* she thinking?'

'Well, I'm sure it wasn't her fault,' Doris said with a sympathetic smile.

Mrs Soames clicked her tongue as though nothing

could be further from the truth.

One thing had led to another and Doris had invited her back to her house for a cup of tea. She'd brought out her best china cups from the dresser but Mrs Soames grimaced as she picked hers up.

'It's chipped,' she complained, her face sour.

'Oh, I am sorry, my dear,' Doris said. 'My Henry chipped that in the garden one summer with his secateurs and I can't bear to part with it. Let me get you another one.'

Doris left the room for a brief moment and that's when Mrs Soames had seen Katherine and Warwick's wedding invitation sitting on the mantelpiece above the fire, her eyes scanning the words.

Cordially invited ... Doris Norris and guest ... Purley Hall, Hampshire.

Mrs Soames's chest had heaved upwards as she clocked it.

'And who is your guest?' she boomed, her mouth a thin line across her face.

Doris had simpered and dithered for a few seconds before finally relenting and inviting Mrs Soames but now, standing outside Winchester train station underneath her National Trust umbrella, she wondered if she'd made the right decision.

'Just look at the time!' Dame Pamela said, fanning herself with a menu. 'For goodness' sake, Dan, go and see if Warwick's all right. We can't have a wedding without the groom!'

Dan nodded and ran up the stairs or rather he *half*-ran because he was now wearing his Regency attire and didn't want to come a cropper in his fine breeches. When he reached Warwick's room, he paused for a moment.

'Keep calm,' he told himself. 'Don't show him that you're anxious. Just play it cool.'

He rapped lightly on the door. After a few seconds had gone by, he knocked again, louder this time. 'Warwick?' He grimaced. His voice had sounded horribly anxious. 'Can I come in?' His hand closed around the door knob and he entered the room.

And there was Warwick – still sat at the dressing table, pen in hand, wearing his old shirt and a pair of jeans.

'Dan!' he said, looking up from his writing.

'Hello,' Dan said, looking at his wrist watch in an attempt to show Warwick the importance of his call. 'You okay?'

'Super,' Warwick said.

'Only, you're not dressed.'

'No,' Warwick said. 'What's the time?'

'It's three o'clock,' Dan said.

'Oh, plenty of time then,' Warwick said and his head bowed down towards his writing again.

Dan gulped. 'Erm, Warwick,' he began uneasily, 'now's really not the time.'

'Not the time for what?'

'For writing a book.'

'I know,' he said, 'but I can't help myself. *With a book he was regardless of time.*'

'Pardon?'

'*Pride and Prejudice* – a reference to Mr Bennet reading but I'm like that when I'm writing,' Warwick said.

'Oh, I see,' Dan said. 'I'm still not used to everyone talking in quotes and I really should be by now.' He paused, waiting for Warwick to pull himself together and realise that he was getting married in about an hour's time. He cleared his throat. 'Don't you think you should be getting dressed?'

Warwick looked up again as if surprised that Dan was still there. 'In a minute,' he said, and returned to his writing.

Dan left the room, an uneasy cocktail of confusion and anxiety flowing through him.

His mobile rang.

'Dan?'

'Robyn?' he said, relieved to hear a friendly voice amongst all of the chaos. 'Is everything okay?'

She paused before answering. 'I'm not sure,' she said.

'What do you mean?'

'I mean, Katherine's been acting strangely. She keeps asking me all these questions about married life and – well – I'm not sure what's going on.'

'Oh my God! Warwick's been acting weirdly too. He's been sitting in his room writing *all* morning. He's not even dressed yet. I can't seem to get through to him.'

'Oh, Dan! What are we going to do? I'm really worried.'

Dan cast his eyes to the ceiling in despair. This was the first time he'd ever been a best man and he had no idea how to cope in such a situation.

'Listen, can you get to the stables?' he asked.

'I think so but I can't be too long. The carriage is arriving in an hour.'

'Meet me there in five minutes, okay?'

'Okay,' Robyn said and hung up.

Leaving the hall a moment later, Dan walked down

the main drive towards the stables. Ordinarily, he would have enjoyed an excuse to get outside and breathe in the warm, sweet smell of the horses but he was feeling too stressed today to take pleasure in such things.

He was the first to arrive in the yard. The horses had all been let out in the fields hours ago and were being taken care of by a teenager in the village called Georgia who was crazy about horses and spent every hour she could in the yard at Purley. Dan walked across to the tack room to check up on things. Everything was in good order just as it should be. Georgia was worth her weight in gold.

It was just as he was looking at his watch and wondering how long Robyn would be when a woman entered the yard. But it wasn't Robyn; it was Carmel Hudson.

'Dan!' she said, her eyes appraising his Regency outfit and her smile informing him that she was very pleased with it. 'Oh, dear. Is this a bad time?'

'Not a bad time,' Dan said, 'just a busy one.'

'I just wanted a quick word really,' she said, 'in private.'

'Oh,' Dan said.

She motioned towards a stable. Dan looked surprised for a moment.

'It's about my riding lessons,' Carmel said, smoothing her hands down her electric blue dress.

'Right,' Dan said, as if it all made perfect sense and he followed her into the stable without thinking that there was anything unusual in that.

'I tried to ring you last night but you weren't answering your phone.'

'We had guests,' Dan explained.

'And you didn't call me back?' she asked, a sulky, teenage-like expression on her face.

'No, sorry. We've got a wedding here today and I'm the best man.'

'I bet you are,' Carmel said, her silky voice slow and provocative and, before Dan knew what was happening, her arms had fastened around his neck and she was leaning up to kiss him.

'Mrs Hud-' his voice was suffocated by another kiss. Dan was, of course, strong enough to fend her off but he was also sensible enough to realise the delicacy of the situation and didn't want to anger her. However, he most certainly did not kiss her back.

'Mrs Hudson – really – '

'I *do* so like a man in costume,' she said.

'Please – stop this!'

'Oh, you are *such* a naughty boy,' she said, slapping him playfully on the bottom when she finally came up from air. 'I've told you a thousand times to call me Carmel.'

Dan ran a hand through his hair. 'Look,' he said, his voice low but serious, 'I'm married. I've got a daughter. I was happy to consider you and your daughter for riding lessons but I think we'd better cancel that now, don't you?'

'You don't want to make an enemy of me, Dan,' she said, inching forward again, her hands now flat on his chest.

'Mrs Hudson, I think you'd better leave.'

'Oh, don't be so melodramatic!' she said and then she smiled her cat-like, taunting smile. 'I won't tell if you won't.'

'Dan?' Robyn's voice called from outside the stable.

Dan pushed Carmel Hudson out of the way. 'Robyn?'

'Oh, there you are!' Robyn said. Unlike Dan, she wasn't yet wearing her wedding outfit but a loosely-fitting blouse and a long skirt, but her hair had been swept back and Dan saw white ribbon threaded through it.

'Robyn, I-' but he didn't have time to explain because Carmel Hudson calmly walked out of the stable in her brilliant blue dress as if she was walking into a Hollywood premiere.

'Oh, is this your little wife, then?' she said, narrowing her eyes as she took in Robyn. 'I see what you mean now, Dan darling.'

Robyn's mouth dropped open.

'Mrs Hudson, I think you'd better leave.'

She sighed dramatically. 'Well, if you insist. You know I'll do anything you want me to.'

Dan and Robyn watched in horrified silence as Carmel Hudson left the stable yard.

'*What* is going on?' Robyn cried as soon as she was out of sight.

'Nothing!' Dan said. 'It was nothing!'

'Then why have you got red lipstick all over your mouth?' Robyn asked, her eyes wide and full of hurt. 'And what did she mean when she said "I see what you mean now, *Dan darling*."'

Dan wiped a hand across his mouth. 'She meant to stir up trouble – that's all. She's been bugging me for days about wanting riding lessons.'

'Was that her on the phone last night?' Robyn asked.

Dan nodded.

'I think she might have rung the cottage too.

Someone rang twice today and hung up when I answered.'

'Oh, Robyn. I'm so sorry.'

'So, what was going on in the stable before I arrived?'

'Nothing. She was doing her best to-' Dan paused.

'To what?'

'To compromise me,' Dan said.

Robyn's eyes were filled with tears now. 'What happened? Did you kiss her?'

'Of *course* I didn't!' he said, running a hand through his hair. 'But it was rather hard to avoid her. She just sort of *lunged* at me.'

'Oh, Dan!' Robyn cried.

'Listen,' he said, his hands reaching out to hold her shoulders, but it was then that Robyn's phone vibrated somewhere in her voluminous skirt.

'Hello?' she said a moment later. 'No, I'm not far away. It's okay. All right.' She hung up and looked at Dan. 'It's Katherine. I've got to get back.'

'Robyn!' Dan shouted after her as she quickly walked away. 'We haven't sorted out what we're going to do about Katherine and Warwick!'

CHAPTER 13

Dan watched helplessly as Robyn walked away from him. What was he going to do? He was meant to be safely ushering Warwick up the aisle but now his own marriage seemed to be in jeopardy. Team that with a bride who seemed to be having second thoughts and a groom who hadn't even got dressed yet and the whole day seemed to be falling apart.

There was only one thing for it, he thought, as he wiped his hand across his mouth once more just to make sure there was no trace left of Carmel Hudson's lipstick. He had to talk to Pammy.

Dame Pamela was sitting in a chair in her bedroom whilst half a can of hairspray was being applied to a very elegant chignon when Dan entered.

'Darling!' she cried. 'Whatever's the matter?'

'Everything,' he said, flopping down on the end of her bed.

Dame Pamela whispered something to the hairdresser who then swiftly left the room.

'Tell me what's going on,' she said, turning her full attention to her little brother, and Dan took a deep breath and began. By the time he finished, his sister's face was creased into a dozen lines of anxiety.

'So,' Dame Pamela said, 'let me see if I've got this right. Katherine's having second thoughts about getting married, Warwick's in some kind of writing trance and seems to have forgotten it's his wedding day and your wife thinks you're having an affair with Carmel Hudson?'

'That's about the measure of things,' Dan said.

'And you want me to do what exactly?'

Dan's hands flew up in the air. '*Any*thing, Pammy!' he said in desperation. 'I don't know what to do! I'm totally lost in all this!'

Dame Pamela reached out and cupped his face in her hands and then she gazed out of the window with a sigh, a thoughtful look on her face.

Dan watched intently. Would she be able to fix the multitudinous problems or was the whole day going to end in disaster? He looked at the little carriage clock on the dressing table. It was half past three. Katherine's carriage was arriving at Horseshoe Cottage in half an hour and the ceremony was meant to be taking place half an hour after that.

'Pammy?' he prompted but she was still gazing out of the window. Finally, she nodded and turned back to him.

'Right,' she began, 'don't worry about Robyn. She's the sweetest girl I've ever met and she'll understand what happened. We all know what Carmel Hudson is like, don't we? I hear she cornered the poor Fedex guy last month. He only asked her to sign for a package.'

Dan sighed.

'*Nobody's* going to blame you for becoming her next victim - least of all Robyn.'

'You didn't see the way she looked at me, Pammy.'

Dame Pamela twisted one of her diamond rings. 'Well, she's probably a bit bruised right now. Most wives are if they see their husband in the clutches of another woman.'

'But it wasn't my fault!' Dan stressed.

'I know but it still happened and you have to make sure that you make Robyn feel secure that she's the only woman in your life.'

'Well, of course she is!' Dan said. 'I'd do anything for her.'

'Then you might have to prove that to her.'

Dan nodded. 'Okay,' he said. 'I'll tell her. I'll show her. I'll do anything. Now, will you talk to Katherine?'

'Well, I'm wondering if I'm really the best person to do that.'

'Of *course* you are!' Dan said, desperation fuelling his voice.

Dame Pamela didn't look convinced. 'You want me to reassure Katherine about the institution of marriage? Do you know how many husbands I've had?'

'No, I've lost count,' Dan said honestly.

'Yes, and I have too,' Dame Pamela said.

'Just talk to her,' he pleaded. 'Katherine and Warwick are meant to be together. Just like Elizabeth and Darcy.'

Dame Pamela nodded. 'Of course,' she said.

'And then will you help me with Warwick?'

'Well, I'll do my best,' she said.

'Thank you!' Dan said, leaping to his feet. 'Now, let's see if I can at least prise Warwick away from his latest novel.'

Robyn had managed to persuade Katherine to get dressed and the two of them were sitting in her bedroom in their gowns. It should have been a moment of great happiness: their hair had been decorated with tiny white rose buds and ribbons and their dresses had turned them into Regency heroines but Katherine had been babbling for the last ten minutes and Robyn was seriously worried.

'What about the assertion that "Happiness in

marriage is entirely a matter of chance",' Katherine asked her maid of honour.

'Katherine, you mustn't take quotes out of context,' Robyn told her.

'But it's absolutely *in* context,' Katherine said.

'I don't think you can read meaning into every single Jane Austen line,' Robyn said. Of course, she did that herself almost every day but she wasn't going to admit that to Katherine in her current mood. 'It's fiction, after all. We don't really know what Jane Austen thought about marriage – not *really*.'

'But she never married,' Katherine said. 'She dedicated herself to her work. Doesn't that tell us all we need to know?'

'But she never met the right man like you did,' Robyn said with an encouraging smile.

'But what if she did and we just don't know about it? What if there was something in one of the letters that Cassandra destroyed? What if she chose her work over a man and I'm making a huge mistake? What if I should be like her and forsake marriage for my work?'

Robyn frowned. She wasn't used to such discussions and it was all becoming too much for her. Katherine seemed so adamant in her opinion and what she'd said was probably the best argument against marriage that a Janeite could come up with.

She looked at Katherine sitting on the edge of the bed in her wedding dress and her heart ached for her because she sincerely believed that there wasn't going to be a wedding today. Jane Austen might have brought Katherine and Warwick together but it seemed as if Katherine was trying to use her favourite author to tear them apart.

CHAPTER 14

Dame Pamela parked her Rolls Royce outside Horseshoe Cottage and walked up the garden path before knocking on the door. It was opened by Robyn a moment later.

'Oh, look at you! You look absolutely breathtaking!' Dame Pamela said.

'Thank goodness you're here,' Robyn said.

'Where's Katherine?'

'Upstairs in our bedroom. I don't know what to do. I think she's talked herself out of marrying Warwick. She keeps quoting Jane Austen and saying work's more important than marriage.'

Dame Pamela shook her head. 'Some people are just too clever for their own good.'

'I didn't know what to say to her.'

Dame Pamela took Robyn's hands in hers. 'Make a nice cup of Earl Grey and I'll go and talk to her.'

Robyn disappeared into the kitchen and Dame Pamela climbed the stairs, holding the long blossom-pink material of her dress in her hands so as not to trip herself up.

'Katherine?' she called.

'Dame Pamela?'

'My dear,' she said as she entered the room. 'Everybody's so worried about you.'

Katherine's dark eyes widened in her pale face. 'Are they?'

Dame Pamela sat down beside her on the bed. 'Now, what's going on?'

Dan rapped loudly on Warwick's door three times before turning the handle and letting himself inside.

'Warwick?' he called, swallowing hard when he realised that there was no sign of the groom. So, this was it, Dan thought. Warwick had run out on his own wedding and it would fall to Dan to inform the bride.

He was just about to flop onto the bed and bury his head in his hands when he heard whistling coming from the bathroom. Dan frowned as he tried to make out the tune and smiled as he realised what it was.

'Here comes the bride!' he said to himself and then he laughed.

'Dan!' Warwick said, emerging from the bathroom fully dressed. 'I was just beginning to worry you weren't going to show up!'

'*You* were worried about *me* not showing up?' Dan said as he stood up, shaking his head. 'I thought you'd done a runner!'

'What?' Warwick cried.

Dan looked completely bamboozled for a moment and just stood there shaking his head for a moment, his hand waving around in the air as he tried to explain himself.

'You were in another world with your writing and you weren't listening to me. I got worried. I guess I panicked. I thought you were having second thoughts.'

'Second thoughts?' Warwick's face fell at the mere idea.

'I was so worried.'

'Oh, dear!' he cried. 'I didn't mean to worry you. I just got a bit hyper with the writing. It's this deadline and I guess it's the adrenalin from all this wedding business. I picked up my pen this morning and couldn't stop.'

Dan ran a hand through his hair and sighed. 'But

we're okay now?'

'I'm dressed, aren't I?'

Dan nodded. 'You are,' he said.

'And Katherine's all ready, I take it?'

'Ah!' Dan said, taking a deep breath. 'We might actually have a problem with the bride.'

Robyn entered the room with three cups of Earl Gray tea on a red lacquered tray.

'Here,' she said.

Dame Pamela and Katherine were sitting on the bed and the scene looked calm, almost convivial, but Katherine's dark eyes were still full of anxiety.

'I've been telling Katherine that there are no guarantees with marriage,' Dame Pamela said, patting the bed beside her.

Robyn sat down. 'No,' she said.

'No guarantees with anything,' she went on. 'One can plan and hope and dream but, in the end, you just have to take one day at a time and make the very best decision you can on that day.'

Katherine nodded. 'But is getting married really the best decision?' she asked, turning to Dame Pamela.

'You seemed to think so,' Dame Pamela said, waving her hand over the fairytale fabric of Katherine's wedding dress.

'Yes,' Katherine said, 'but I'm not so sure now. What if I fail at this? I'm not very good at failing but what if I disappoint Warwick? What if I find I'm terrible as a wife. What–'

Dame Pamela rested a hand on her shoulder. 'Katherine – you can't live worrying about what might or might not happen in the future.'

'But that's how I've always lived. I've always planned things – my lessons, my books, my career – and I've always been in control but I don't feel in control of this and it scares me.'

Dame Pamela looked at Robyn who was biting her lip most ferociously. 'What shall we do?' she mouthed. Dame Pamela gave a little shrug and sipped her tea.

Warwick was pacing up and down like a caged beast.

'You'll wear a hole in Pammy's Axminster if you keep this up much longer,' Dan warned him.

'What if she doesn't show up?' Warwick said. 'Is it me? Is she thinking I'm going to mess up again?'

'You're not going to mess up again,' Dan said. 'Why would you?'

'Because it just seems to be what I do around Katherine.'

Dan shook his head. 'That's nonsense.'

'It's not. I'm a clumsy, babbling idiot compared to her. No wonder she's having second thoughts.'

'I'm sure she's not. She's probably just a bit nervous. All brides get nervous.'

'Do they?'

'Yes!' Dan said. 'It's also their prerogative to run late. That's probably what's going on here. There's been a minor crisis with the dress or the flowers or something.'

'You think?'

Dan nodded. 'I'm positive,' he said, swallowing hard and trying to keep calm. 'So we'll just take care of things this end, okay?'

Warwick stopped pacing and looked at Dan.

'Okay,' he said. 'Let's get on with things our end.'

'Good,' Dan said.

'I take it you've got the rings,' Warwick said with a grin.

Dan laughed and patted the neat pocket in his trousers but his face fell as his fingers dug around inside it.

'Dan?' Warwick said, his voice full of fear.

Dan looked up in horror. 'There's only one,' he said, cursing under his breath.

'Don't mess about, Dan!' Warwick said. 'I know you've got the rings.'

Dan shook his head, the colour draining from his face. 'There's one missing,' he said, taking the remaining ring from his pocket. It was the larger of the two – the groom's ring.

'So, let me get this straight,' Warwick said, doing his best to keep calm, 'the bride might have done a runner and now we've lost her ring?'

CHAPTER 15

The guests were gathering in the library. Lily was sitting in the front row looking thoroughly miserable, Mia and Shelley who had befriended Katherine's good pal Chrissie were two rows behind, Roberta and Rose were sitting in the middle and Doris Norris and Mrs Soames were beside them. Warwick's agent, Nadia Sparks, was also there, looking anxiously at her watch and wondering when the champagne would be served. All of them but Lily had chosen a costume from Dame Pamela's collection and looked as pretty as hummingbirds in shades of blue, pink, green and yellow.

'It's all so beautiful!' Roberta gushed as she looked around the room. She was wearing a shell-pink dress with a matching bonnet. 'I do so love lilies!'

Mrs Soames, wearing a brilliant striped emerald and silver gown, huffed and shook her head. 'Messy flowers. The pollen drops everywhere and stains. I prefer a nice sensible chrysanthemum. You know where you are with a chrysanthemum.'

'I don't think you can beat roses,' Doris Norris said. She was wearing a dress the colour of bluebells which was edged with gold around the neckline and sleeves.

'Well, I've always been partial to a rose, it has to be said,' Rose said with a smile. She was wearing a dazzling sunshine-yellow dress with puffed sleeves and a very elegant pair of long gloves.

'Thorns,' Mrs Soames said. 'A chrysanthemum won't cut you to shreds.'

Doris caught Roberta's eye and they exchanged knowing smiles. Mrs Soames, it seemed, even found something to complain about when it came to flowers.

'Shouldn't something have happened by now?' Rose said a moment later.

Mrs Soames looked at her watch. 'By my calculation, the groom should be standing at the top of the aisle.'

'Where is he, then?' Rose asked, looking around. 'Do you think anything's wrong?'

'Knowing this place,' Mrs Soames said, '*something* will have gone wrong!'

Warwick and Dan were running down the driveway towards the stable block.

'I think I know where the ring could be,' Dan said. 'I got in a tussle with a woman from the village in one of the stables.'

'What?' Warwick cried from behind him.

'She just launched herself at me,' Dan said. 'It was dreadful. She wanted riding lessons for herself and her daughter. Well, I thought she did. Turns out she probably just wanted a roll in the hay.'

They arrived at the stable where the incident had taken place and the two men started to scour the floor.

'So, this is the scene of the crime?' Warwick said.

'There's nothing going on,' Dan told him.

'It's okay – I believe you. Thousands wouldn't mind!'

'No. I think Robyn might be one of them. She walked in on us.'

'Oh, lord!' Warwick said.

'This isn't turning out to be my day,' Dan said.

They continued hunting around the stable, gently

poking and kicking around in the straw.

'Watch your trousers,' Dan said when he saw Warwick bending down.

'Katherine will kill me if I get married looking like a scarecrow. She's expecting Mr Darcy not Worzel Gummidge.'

'God, I'm so sorry, Warwick. What a nightmare.'

'It's okay. Don't panic. It's not your fault,' he said.

'Of all the things to happen,' Dan said.

'We'll find it,' Warwick assured him, 'and, no doubt, I'll probably write about this one day. It would make a terrific scene for one of my books.'

'Here!' Dan said a second later. 'Oh, it's a Quality Street wrapper. I just saw something gold.'

They went on searching.

'I've got it!' Warwick said a minute later.

'Oh, thank goodness!' Dan said. 'But we'd better give it a wash before you pop it on her finger.'

They returned to the hall and retreated upstairs where they washed the ring in Warwick's ensuite with warm water and a bar of Pears soap.

'Well, we've got the ring,' Warwick said. 'What about the bride?'

Dan got his phone out and rang Robyn. A moment later, he looked up at Warwick and the wounded look in his eyes told him all he needed to know.

'She's not coming, is she?' Warwick said.

'They don't know,' Dan said.

Warwick looked totally lost for a moment but then he seemed to leap a foot in the air. 'Get me some paper!' he cried.

'Warwick, mate,' Dan said, 'now isn't the time to write your novel.'

'Not my novel,' Warwick said. 'I need to write to Katherine!'

Dan turned to the left and then to the right, desperately searching for something Warwick could write on. 'The dressing table drawer!' he shouted.

Warwick ran across the room and opened it, discovering a neat pile of writing paper with 'Purley Hall' embossed in gold across the top and a collection of envelopes.

Reaching for his fountain pen, Warwick wrote.

'Right,' he said a moment later, blowing on the ink before folding the paper and placing it carefully into an envelope. 'Can you get this to Katherine for me?'

'Of course,' Dan said, surprised by the speed at which Warwick had written his letter to Katherine. Didn't he want to spend more time on it? Didn't he want this opportunity to pour his heart out to her? But Dan didn't question him because he didn't think that went with the job description of best man. Instead, he left the room in hast and sprinted down the driveway. His heart was racing madly. He'd never known a day like it. Even when he thought back to his stressful job in London, he could honestly say that nothing could compare to today.

Once at Horseshoe Cottage, Dan knocked loudly on the door and, a moment later, Robyn answered.

'Dan!' she said in surprise.

'Is Katherine still here?'

'Yes,' Robyn said, 'but we don't know what's happening. Pammy's with her now and her Uncle Ned is pacing around in the kitchen like a lost thing.'

'I've got a letter from Warwick. Will you give it to her?'

'Of course. I'll take it up right now.' Robyn looked

up at her husband. 'Are you to wait for an answer?'

'Oh, I didn't ask. Perhaps I should.'

'Okay,' she said, and an awkward moment passed between them but there wasn't time to discuss what was going on with them right now because this was Katherine and Warwick's day and they had to put that first.

Lily Lawton looked at her watch for the fifth time in as many minutes. Shouldn't her brother be here by now? The congregation was getting anxious with people whispering and looking around but too polite to ask what was happening. But Lily knew what was happening. Her message had got through to Warwick, hadn't it? He'd changed his mind about this whole marriage business, realising that his sister was right and that he was better off as a bachelor.

Lily sighed in relief. She'd paid for a new navy trouser suit for the wedding but it was a small price to pay for the happiness of her little brother. He'd come to see she was right in time and that he didn't need to put a ring on a woman's finger in order to love her and Katherine would forgive him if she truly loved him.

She shook her head as she turned around and saw the sea of brilliantly coloured Regency gowns behind her. She'd been offered a costume when she'd arrived and had uttered something very unAustensian. Honestly, these people lived on a different planet, didn't they? And the sooner she and her brother got away from it all, the better.

'Katherine?' Robyn said as she entered the bedroom. 'I've got a letter for you from Warwick.'

Katherine's eyes widened at this declaration. 'Is he here?'

'Dan delivered it,' Robyn said, handing the envelope to her and exchanging an anxious look with Dame Pamela.

Katherine opened it and unfolded the paper inside and silently read the words written there in Warwick's writing.

Six words. Just six. But the right six.

Katherine's hand dropped into her lap for a moment and then she looked up, and her eyes suddenly seemed to dance with light.

'Robyn – *help* me!' she said, leaping up from the bed with the letter still clutched in her hand.

'Are we going to a wedding, then?' Robyn asked.

'Of *course* we are! Oh, what was I thinking of, Robyn? Where did all those doubts come from? I must have been mad!'

Robyn looked at Dame Pamela and they suddenly burst into laughter.

'Oh, Katherine!' Dame Pamela exclaimed, hugging the bride to her rapturously.

'Pammy – would you tell Dan to let Warwick know we're on our way?' Robyn said.

'Yes, of course.'

'He's downstairs.'

'And ask Uncle Ned to come upstairs,' Katherine said. 'He must be wondering what on earth is going on.'

Dame Pamela nodded and left the room and Katherine and Robyn stood there staring at one another.

'What must you think of me?' Katherine whispered.

'I think you're wonderful,' Robyn said honestly, 'and I think you've made the best decision in the world.'

Katherine nodded, tears shining brilliantly in her eyes. 'I have, haven't I?'

Robyn nodded. 'Now, let's get you to your groom!'

CHAPTER 16

The Regency-style open-top carriage looked perfect and Robyn helped Katherine in to it before handing her the bouquet of white roses.

She then climbed in and sat opposite Katherine and her Uncle Ned. It felt like a wonderful extravagance to have hired a carriage and horses to travel so short a distance but when else in life could you get away with such a thing? If a woman couldn't indulge herself on her wedding day then when could she?

It looked so smart with its black and brown leather interior and shiny brass fittings and the two chestnut horses who had been groomed so that they almost shone. The driver and assistant were equally smart in navy suit and tails and hats and they set off for Purley Hall at a smart pace.

Uncle Ned took his niece's hand in his and squeezed it. 'You look wonderful,' he told her. 'Absolutely wonderful!'

'You do too,' Katherine said, noticing his fabulous costume which included a wonderful purple cravat and matching waistcoat. His silver hair was short and neat and his round glasses gave his round face a quizzical look. 'I hope I didn't worry you before.'

Uncle Ned cleared his throat and straightened his cravat. 'Well, I did wear a bit of a trench in Robyn's kitchen floor with all the pacing but this is your day, Katherine, and it's important that you made the right decision,' he said, patting her hand.

Katherine smiled up at him as the carriage turned into the driveway of Purley Hall.

Since arriving back with Dan and imparting the good news to Warwick who had thumped Dan on the back until he'd coughed and squeezed Dame Pamela until she'd begged for mercy, the dame had straightened and primped her blossom-pink Regency gown and finished her outfit with a single string of pearls around her neck. It was incredibly understated for her but she knew that this wasn't her day to take centre stage – that honour went to Katherine. Still, she hadn't been able to resist a great pink feather worn at a jaunty angle in her chignon.

She was thrilled to see that so many of the guests were in costume but, then again, most of them were Janeites and they never needed much encouragement to don a bonnet or a pelisse. But there was a funny woman in the front row who didn't really look like a woman at all in her crisp navy trouser suit. Dame Pamela wrinkled her nose. She did like women to *look* like women. It seemed a pity, too, because she was very attractive with her Audrey Hepburn-like hair and neat features.

'Lily!' Dame Pamela said to herself as she realised who the woman was and she went to greet her instantly. 'My dear,' she said, clasping her hand in delight. 'How lovely to meet you.'

Lily looked surprised but returned her host's smile. 'And you too, Dame Pamela,' she said graciously.

'I'm so excited about today. You must be so proud of Warwick.'

'Well, I-'

'And there he is!' The congregation turned as one as Warwick and Dan entered the library and a soft round of applause rippled through the room. Lily's mouth dropped open and she stared aghast as her brother came to stand beside her.

'I thought you weren't coming,' she said.

'What?' Warwick said, turning to face his sister in surprise.

'I thought you'd seen sense and had jilted Katherine.'

Warwick looked absolutely horrified. 'You thought I'd do that?'

'Well, I was hoping you would.'

'Lily,' he said in a hushed tone, 'Katherine is the love of my life. She's my whole world now and, if you can't see that, then perhaps you'd better leave.'

Lily looked dumbstruck for a moment but then swallowed hard and took a deep breath. 'Sorry,' she said in a tiny voice.

'Pardon?' Warwick said.

'I said I'm sorry!' she said, just as the string quartet had stopped playing to change their music. Her voice carried forth across the congregation and Lily blushed to her ears.

'Good!' Warwick whispered back. 'Katherine is going to be my wife and your sister-in-law and the sooner you embrace that, the better,' he said, leaning forward to kiss Lily's cheek.

After the photographer had taken about two hundred photographs of Katherine arriving in the carriage and standing in the entrance hall, the bride entered the library. The string quartet were playing some Vivaldi as Uncle Ned walked Katherine up the aisle and Katherine gasped at the sight that greeted her.

The library at Purley was a wondrous sight at any time but today, full of friendly faces in a splendid array of costumes and with the mingled scent of lilies and roses, it took Katherine's breath away. She recognised many of the faces smiling at her – dear friends from her Oxfordshire village, colleagues from St Bridget's College and fellow Janeites from the Austen conferences. Even her future sister-in-law was smiling, Katherine couldn't help noticing.

And there, standing at the top of the aisle, was Warwick.

He turned to look at her and his eyes were so full of love that Katherine was reminded of the moment in the 1995 adaptation of *Pride and Prejudice* where Mr Darcy is watching Elizabeth Bennet as she turns the pages of music for his sister Georgiana and the tenderest, most passionate look is exchanged between the two of them and you know that they will be together forever.

Uncle Ned walked Katherine to her groom, played his part and then took a step back and Warwick reached out to hold Katherine's hand. She took in the sky-blue cravat he was wearing and the fabulously ornate cream and gold waistcoat teamed with a dark jacket and dark breeches.

'You look beautiful,' he whispered.

Katherine smiled up at him. 'I got your note,' she told him.

He grinned. 'I guessed.'

Robyn, who was standing behind Katherine, now took her bouquet. She'd heard the brief exchange between them and was quite desperate to know the contents of Warwick's letter. What had he said to her to have made her so very sure so very suddenly?

But it wasn't very hard to guess which six words Warwick had written to Katherine – not very hard to guess for a Janeite – because Warwick had chosen Captain Wentworth's words to Anne Elliot in *Persuasion* from the most romantic letter ever written.

"*I am half agony, half hope.*"

CHAPTER 17

Half-way through the ceremony, Dame Pamela stood up and gave a reading which was, of course, the final paragraph from Jane Austen's *Emma* and the congregation nodded and sighed with happiness as she read the words 'the small band of true friends who witnessed the ceremony were fully answered in the perfect happiness of the union.'

Dan caught Robyn's eye and mouthed the word 'sorry' across the aisle but she cast her eyes to the floor and refused to look at him. He swallowed hard.

When the moment came to exchange rings, Dan stepped forward and shared an amused look with Warwick which, luckily, nobody else saw otherwise questions would surely have been asked and, before they knew it, the registrar declared that Warwick and Katherine were husband and wife and a great cheer went up from the congregation and Warwick leaned in to kiss his bride.

'Is that straw in your hair?' Katherine said as they were asked to sign the register.

Warwick's hand flew up to his head. 'I er –'

'How on *earth* did you get straw in your hair?'

'I just took a quick trip to the stables,' he said. 'Isn't it meant to be good luck to pat a grey horse on your wedding day?'

'Is it?' Katherine said. 'It's the first I've heard about it.'

The wedding party were just making their way outside for photographs when Robyn took Katherine to one side and adjusted her hair.

'There, that's better,' she said with a smile. 'You

almost lost a rosebud after that kiss of Warwick's!'

Suddenly, Katherine grabbed Robyn's arm as she spotted a buxom woman in a brilliant emerald-green and silver dress.

'Robyn?'

'Yes?'

'What's Mrs Soames doing here?' Katherine asked in alarm.

'Oh,' Robyn said, 'I meant to warn you. I'm afraid Doris Norris invited her – she was kind of pressured into it from what I can gather.'

Katherine stared in amazement as Mrs Soames caught her eye. She was heading right towards her. There would be no avoiding her.

'Oh, goodness!' Katherine cursed under her breath. Of all the days to have a confrontation with Mrs Soames.

'Ah, Dr Roberts,' Mrs Soames began, her enormous chest heaving itself towards the startled bride, 'there's something I am compelled to tell you.'

'Really, Mrs Soames? Are you sure it has to be now only I'm a little busy,' Katherine said, making to move away but Mrs Soames stopped her, laying a fat hand on the bride's arm.

'Yes, I simply *must* tell you,' she went on, 'that you look absolutely *beautiful!*' Mrs Soames said with just the hint of a smile warming her large face.

Katherine blinked in shock. Was that a compliment she'd just been given? By Mrs Soames? The woman who did nothing but find fault with the world and then inform ever single resident of it?

Mrs Soames nodded at the bemused Katherine and then turned to leave.

'Did I just imagine that?' she asked, turning to her

maid of honour.

Robyn's face broke into a huge smile. 'Well, I never!' she said. 'Mr Knightley said "Surprises are foolish things" but I think that was rather wonderful!'

The little temple on the island had been dressed with pink and white roses and sky-blue ribbons and Katherine and Warwick posed for photographs.

'You look so radiant,' Warwick told Katherine in between shots.

'And you look like the perfect gentleman,' she said.

'Better than Mr Darcy?' he dared to ask.

'*So* much better,' she said, leaning up to kiss him.

'Perfect!' the photographer shouted.

'I do love you, Mrs Lawton,' he said a moment later.

'And I love you,' she said, smiling up at him.

'Good. Now, let's eat!'

The starter was white soup from the recipe taken from the cook book of Jane Austen's good friend, Martha Lloyd. It also had the honour of featuring in Chapter 11 of *Pride and Prejudice* so it was a truly fitting dish for the wedding breakfast.

Roast beef had been chosen for the main course and a simple dessert of strawberries and cream in honour of *Emma* was received with much delight by everyone.

The wedding speeches followed including a surprise one by Dame Pamela.

'I have the most wonderful announcement!' she said, tapping her champagne flute for everybody's attention. 'One of our lovely guests - Mia Castle – who helped to make Katherine's stunning wedding dress, has just had a phone call. Her sister, Sarah, whom some of you met at our Christmas conference, has just had a baby girl.

A great cheer went up, followed by a huge round of applause.

'And her name is Elinor Elizabeth!' Dame Pamela continued.

Lily rolled her eyes. 'Another Austen addict?' she asked her brother.

'Of course!' Warwick said. 'You're quite outnumbered here. You should just swallow your pride-' he paused, '*and* prejudice and join ranks!' He laughed loudly at his own joke and Lily flushed with embarrassment and wondered if it would be rude if she left early.

It wasn't until the dancing began that Dan finally got to speak to Robyn.

'I've been trying to talk to you all day,' he said as he led her out onto the dance floor.

'Well, I've been kept busy,' she said.

'Of course,' he said, holding her tiny body next to his as the music changed to a slow dance. 'You do know that I never encouraged Mrs Hudson, don't you?' he said.

Robyn didn't reply.

'Robyn!' he said. 'Are you listening to me?' They stopped dancing and stared at one another. 'I would never *ever* do anything like that to you. You're my whole life now. You and Cassie. I'd never put that in danger.' He stroked a long curly strand of hair which had escaped from her hairdo and kissed her forehead so tenderly that it brought tears to Robyn's eyes.

'I guess I'll have to get used to being married to a

man that other women find attractive,' she said.

'And what about you?' Dan said.

'What do you mean?' she asked.

'Other men are attracted to you,' he said.

'No, they're not!' she said, sounding outraged.

'No? What about Uncle Ned?'

'Katherine's Uncle Ned?' she cried.

Dan nodded. 'I saw the way he was eyeing up your Jennifer Ehle cleavage!'

'Dan!' she cried, slapping his arm. Honestly, she really was going to have to stop him from watching Jane Austen adaptations.

On the other side of the dance floor, near to where Doris Norris and Roberta were executing some alarming moves, Katherine and Warwick had their arms wrapped around each other and their foreheads touching.

'Warwick,' she said.

'Yes?'

She bit her lip, not quite knowing how to say what she wanted to say. 'I'm so sorry I-' she paused.

'Nearly jilted me?'

'Made you wait!' she said. 'I did *not* jilt you!'

'There's no need to apologise,' he said.

'But I feel awful that I put you through that.'

He sighed and stroked her cheek. 'We all get a little nervous,' he said. 'I nearly didn't show up myself.'

'Warwick!' she cried but his laughter made her laugh too.

CHAPTER 18

The happiest days of our lives always pass the quickest and so it was with Katherine and Warwick's wedding day. After the dancing, the moment had come to throw the bridal bouquet and the guests joined the happy couple in the entrance hall of Purley where the bride and groom climbed the grand staircase together, stopping six steps up and surveying the crowd below them.

Katherine took one last breath of the scented white roses and then turned her back before launching the bouquet into the air. A great cheer went up when it was discovered who had caught it.

'Oh!' Doris Norris cried. '*Oh!*'

The honeymoon was in Lyme Regis. Katherine and Warwick had debated whether to book something wonderfully exotic like Hawaii or the Seychelles but, in the end, the two of them couldn't think of anywhere more romantic than the bit of English coastline where their beloved Jane had been inspired to set *Persuasion*.

So, they'd booked the best room at Kay Ashton's Wentworth House and enjoyed picnics in the Dorset and Devon countryside, fossil hunting on the Jurassic coast and a visit to Montacute House which had starred as Colonel Brandon's home in the 1995 adaptation of *Sense and Sensibility*.

'I want to come here for *all* my honeymoons,' Warwick said as they walked, hand in hand, along the harbour towards the famous Cobb.

'What?' Katherine cried.

'We *are* going to renew our vows every few years,

aren't we?' he said with a naughty grin.

'You mean, you'd go through all that *again?*' Katherine said, a frown of disbelief etched on her forehead.

They stopped walking and Warwick turned to face her. 'For you, I'd go through *any*thing!' he said and, taking her face in his hands and kissing her passionately, she truly believed that he would.

***

ABOUT THE AUTHOR

Victoria Connelly was brought up in Norfolk and studied English literature at Worcester University before becoming a teacher. After getting married in a medieval castle in the Yorkshire Dales and living in London for eleven years, she moved to rural Suffolk where she lives with her artist husband and a mad Springer spaniel and ex-battery hens.

Her first novel, *Flights of Angels*, was published in Germany and made into a film. Victoria and her husband flew out to Berlin to see it being filmed and got to be extras in it.

Five of her novels have been Kindle bestsellers.

If you'd like to contact Victoria or sign up for her newsletter about future releases, visit her website www.victoriaconnelly.com.

She's also on Facebook and Twitter @VictoriaDarcy

ALSO BY VICTORIA CONNELLY

Austen Addicts Series
A Weekend with Mr Darcy
The Perfect Hero
published in the US as Dreaming of Mr Darcy
Mr Darcy Forever
Christmas with Mr Darcy

Other Fiction
Molly's Millions
The Runaway Actress
Wish You Were Here
Flights of Angels
Unmasking Elena Montella
Three Graces
It's Magic (A compilation volume: Flights of Angels,
Unmasking Elena Montella and Three Graces)

Short Story Collections
One Perfect Week and other stories
The Retreat and other stories
Postcard from Venice and other stories

Non-fiction
Escape to Mulberry Cottage

Children's Adventure
Secret Pyramid

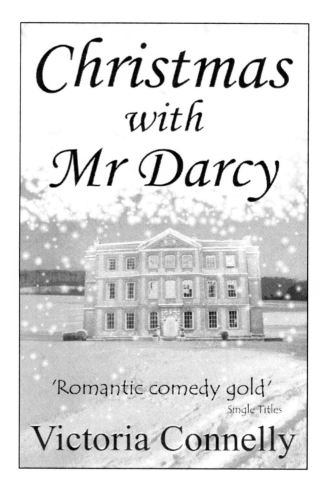

Christmas
with
Mr Darcy

'Romantic comedy gold'
Single Titles

Victoria Connelly

Out Now

CPSIA information can be obtained at www.ICGtesting.com
Printed in the USA
LVOW07s1618250215

428338LV00001B/37/P